2.49

Dan Clements joined the Royal M
to serve in Afghanistan, includ
Helmand and work as an intellige
Forces. He left the Marines in 2008, aged 24, and now lives in London. *what will remain* is his first novel

what will remain

Dan Clements

SILVERTAIL BOOKS • *London*

Published in the UK by Silvertail Books Ltd in 2016

www.silvertailbooks.com

Copyright © Dan Clements 2016
1

Typeset by Elaine Sharples

ISBN 978-1-909269-316

what will remain

Life, to be sure,
Is nothing much to lose,
But young men think it is,
And we were young.
              A. E. Housman

and I picked my face up from the dirt, blinking, and then the hollow square at Bastion with the Hercules tracking low overhead and the chaplain's incantation they shall not grow old and a cleansing flame of sunset that turns the hillranges to blackness, and afterwards the return to operations and there was only that urgency to stay alive and to look after my men and to do what still needed to be done and everything else buried in that deep and forbidden part; learning that something so terrible could be borne out of something as prosaic and senseless as an old gang feud, whew that had been a bitter fucking mouthful to swallow, and I had once seen a factory worker with his hand all chewed up in one of the machines and I eventually came to think of the war in the same way: industrial and random; and it still puts me swinging on my toes to think that the only things I carry with me now, the only real proof that I was ever there at all, are those moments come unstuck from the narrative arc of bravery and heroism and dying for a cause we were sold wholesale as kids; whilst everything else was lost in the pitiless wash of time and forgetfulness it was only those fractured, splintered pieces that bloomed in the most quiet and most hidden places; memories that patchwork my eyelids when I sleep at night; a strange and poignant and fearful heritage:

a policeman spraying blood and bone off the road with a fire hose, the water washing into the ditches in thin pink sheets; and the sound of the women crying, not so much crying out of grief I think, when I see them, when they come to me, more like crying for the fucking cheapness of it all

This couldn't really have come at a worse time, what with the op up north and the Brigadier and CO overseeing the final phase. It's a typical Karzai move: all very knee-jerk, all very reactive. Guaranteed to make all the right headlines and placate all the right people with absolutely zero consideration for the long game.

Thornton drew his lips in and put one hand through his hair. Every sentence he spoke had the polish of an idea overheard or something already said many times before. I waited for him to continue.

As I'm sure you can imagine, the team in Kabul are currently running around like their arses are on fire. By all accounts the Ambassador himself is virtually apoplectic. Trust Karzai to wait until the precise moment our diplomatic architecture is more thinly spread than it has been at any time in the last six months to drop *this* little political bombshell. It's quite, quite wonderful in its own way: devoid of reason and good sense and yet somehow thoroughly charming and Afghan in its execution. – Smiling, a fatherly draw of breath – And so I've scheduled an impromptu meeting with our newly appointed Governor Achakzai at fourteen hundred this afternoon. A successful visit now, with the situation is at its most volatile, should allow us to steady things until we are afforded the time and breathing space to formulate a more considered, a more…appropriate response.

And you'd like me to organise an escort patrol out to the governor's compound?

That's part of it, yes. The pitch I gave the Ambassador this morning is that I would go along to sell Achakzai the big idea. Get him buying in piecemeal into the various threads of the wider strategy we've been progressively weaving together. We will have Ms Cummings on hand to discuss the quick impact projects and the aid packages and the rest of the development bollocks she's so very good at peddling. We were obviously also hoping to have the Brigadier along to add some military gravitas and heavy brass to the proceedings. But given the lie of the land it may be necessary for you to attend as a military representative. Should inspire some of the old warrior camaraderie in Achakzai to have a young, strapping British officer like yourself in attendance, don't you think? Nothing to worry about in any case: you won't be expected to indulge in any deep and meaningful political tête-à-tête. Just give him the stock phrases about pushing the security envelope and holding ground for reconstruction and winning consent. All that hearts and minds stuff you fellows do so well when you're not having a jolly old time stabbing things with your bayonets.

He fixed me this look that was somehow stern and playful and not quite either of those things. A man accustomed to having what he does not say and what he does not express weighted with equal care to that which he does. He held my eye line and let the quiet sit.

With all due respect sir, I'm not sure I have the authority to act as any type of representative, least of all in such a...in such a politically sensitive scenario.

Nonsense. Besides, I've obtained the colonel's permission. He recommended you personally. Something about you being one of the bright young thrusters of your class. I'm sure a man of your calibre appreciates the kind of professional strides one can make off the back of a fortuitous turn of events such as we are privy to today.

He sank back into his chair, turning a pencil like a parade baton between his fingers.

Leaders, captain, are forged in the crucible of chaos and chance.

Pause.

If the colonel's happy, then I'm happy.

Good. Excellent. This is a hugely important day for us. I make no bones about that. Achakzai is a bitter old crow and no doubt Karzai will have already filled his head with all sorts of nonsense about British so-called imperial aspirations in Helmand. You know the sort. It's important that we connect with him early on. Soothe him. Reassure him. Afghans aren't a difficult people to placate if you can learn how to endure their anachronisms. Learn to lever them to your advantage.

The old governor had only been in the job six, maybe eight months, but it would be a stretch to say his removal caught us completely cold. He had been a career politician plucked from some comfortable chancellorship up north and ushered hurriedly into post amidst a fleeting spell of diplomatic consensus, where there was much earnest excited talk of this man uniting the people and this man bringing together our military and our political and our economic strategies and this man shepherding in reconcilable elements of the insurgency and many other slogans then circulating the bars of Kabul. Only things hadn't worked out that way. The history of the province had already carved out a trajectory of its own and that trajectory was wrought by blood and law and phantoms. The history of the province was closefaced: it belonged solely to the Pashtun.

First the mullahs had begun to abandon the monthly shuras in Lashkar Gah. The new school the Danish civil-military teams had been funding in the north of the city was torched and the next day the farmers had leaned into their hoes and squinted at the blackened walls smoking against the midday sky. Then in late spring the fields grew fat and bright with poppy, and the American with the ivory pistol and the sun-bleached Leonard Skynard vest had told me goddamn I ain't never seen this much of a haul, there ain't no way we can pull up four thousand hectares of this shit in time for the loya jirga, goddamn no way, not even if we seize uppa whole fleet of planes and spray the fuckers. Except none of this was what really counted. It took a police warrant and a sack of processed opium the size of a mule to get the governor before him dismissed. What really counted was that this governor was a stranger to the province and that his father had been a stranger and that his father's father had been a stranger.

Finally Karzai tired of this generational outsider. The Ambassador was summoned and the charge sheet of mullahs and schools and poppies and fighting was brought against him and the governor was finished. Diplomats licked their wounds over canapés and tepid sauvignon blanc many hundreds of miles from the relief helicopter that was easing its belly into a courtyard in an anonymous corner of the city. In Helmand politics plays out in one of two ways: the Pashtun man favours his brother and punishes his enemy and his brothers become many and the whole thing sinks into a notional stability and every type of corruption, inshallah. The outsider is cut adrift.

It was early still. Out in the yard the gravel shone like polished bonechina and the sunlight was cold and clean and mannered and you could still feel all the rich false promise of the day bristling in your lungs.

I followed the plastic lattice boardwalk past the accommodation pods and the disused mortar shelter and the sign pointing northwest that read Plymouth 2435m and underneath: Bandit Country 4m. Bonzo was outside the gym hanging from the pull-up bar, his sports vest painted to his skin.

Have the lads kitted up and ready for orders in two hours please. We've got a run down to the governor's compound first thing this afternoon. Two VIPs and a terp along for the ride.

Roger that boss. Anything interesting?

Hakim was shipped out early this morning.

He's gone? How come?

The usual bullshit politics mate. Barely had time to let the doors hit him on the arse on the way out by the sound of things. Looks like I might get first dibs giving the new guy the military angle.

You're briefing the new governor?

Yeah.

Today?

Yeah.

Pause.

Fuck.

Yeah.

We assembled after lunch over mugs of grey coffee and battered patrol maps of the city, the tented walls buffeting and exhaling against a flash duststorm that was huffing through camp. Thornton and Cummings arrived late and sat at the back while the company intelligence officer briefed us on another suspicious white Toyota that had been sighted in the city. That day's was a pick-up. Jacko put up his hand and asked do you know how many fucking white trucks there are around here? Laughter. The intelligence officer shrugged his shoulders apologetically. I'm just giving you what I've got. After the intelligence brief I went through my orders sheet very carefully, very deliberately. We ran over our basic actions-on plans in the event of a contact, plans we have rehearsed with such regularity that when I nominate one of the marines to remind the team on what to do if we get hit from behind he plays it back to me word-for-word. Kind of rhythmic, disinterested, sing-song monotone. It makes me think of learning my tables as a kid. Ambush from side or rear: return fire and drive through the contact. Ambush from the side or rear: return fire and drive through the contact.

Thornton cleared his throat and stood and asked if I wouldn't mind letting him say a few words. I paused, Bonzo firing me a discreet *how the fuck should I know* kind of shrug from where he was seated. I stood to one side and offered up the lectern and returned to my seat and I swilled cold coffee against the roof of my mouth and tapped one foot impatiently against the decking. Thornton steadied himself at the lectern and studied the papers there briefly, as if gathering himself. His shirt was open to the chest and damp from the collar down in a fat wishbone Y. When he looked up again he spoke about it being a rare privilege to have an audience with the men at the sharp end of the war. That it was an honour to speak with undisguised admiration to those who turned the dry soundbites of policy into action and doing at great personal cost. He spoke about the importance of the day ahead, about how this was a turning point for the province, about how the tremors from its impact would be felt long after the events of the day were forgotten, and that our role here in the city was nonetheless critical for it being perhaps repetitive or routine on occasion and far from the field of battle of the popular imagination. He spoke to us of riding the turning tide of history and how Afghanistan and the free world owed us a debt of gratitude for our service and sacrifice. And it was hard to deny the charm he held: his easy grace with words and the way he carried his authority with an affected lightness of touch that made his smile seem like an important gesture casually bestowed. The way he made pantomime and empty phrases ring with the heroic and the timeless.

Thank you for your time, gentlemen.

The marines were quiet as he left. A quiet lost somewhere between lip-bitten *yeah cheers easy* cynicism and this subtle smoulder of pride that was almost audacious in its innocence. A heightened sense of those twin conflicting instincts that seemed to define the character and coda of nearly every marine I ever knew.

Bonzo leaned over to me muttering. That guy could sell syphilis to a whore.

We carried our rifles and our helmets and our webbing and our daysacks across the compound and into the loading bay. The heat from my chest and torso panting out of the body armour in musky wet breaths with each step. The phones were still down by the time we were due to head out. I let myself think of *her*, a glimpse, something stolen, and then I shut everything off and put it away in that place where my other life ended and the rest of me began. Learning to dip in and out of different lives was something most of us mastered early on. It was a hell of a way to keep you on top of your game during deployment. On those early days when you were silently homesick like you couldn't believe and those difficult third and fourth months when it felt like you might never make it back anyway. It was pretty ruthless, living hand-to-mouth like that on whatever scraps of hope and resolve you found going spare. No one ever said what that sort of living might do to us once the war was over. Not unless you count the end-of-tour issue laminate welfare cards imploring us to TALK to our friends and families and to LISTEN to their experiences (they will have struggled too) and ESTABLISH A ROUTINE (do not self-medicate).

Four Snatch Land Rovers were lined up against the high walls of Hesco that formed a two-lane channel leading up to the guard box and out of camp. Jonas was checking boxes of smoke grenades off on a clipboard. Tait stood chest-high out of the rear wagon passing down crates of water into the cabin, the square Kevlar roof flaps folded outwards like an opened gift box. I stood watching. My fingers brushed over the surface of my webbing pouches in a clockwise motion around my waist: magazines one-two-three-four, check, cleaning kit, grenade grenade smoke grenade sundries, check, water bottle, emergency rations, head torch, magazines five-six-seven-eight. The tab of each pouch double-closed to keep the lids from popping open (one, two, three, four, five, six, seven, check), the yolk and strapping warped intimately to the contours of my abdomen.

(sapphire zero this is sapphire three radio check over)

Checking you haven't forgotten your house keys, captain? Thornton snapped himself into his blue armour. A half-smile curling at the edges.

(sapphire three this is sapphire zero good to me over)

Sorry? Oh this. The routine. – Pause – Force of habit.

He raised an eyebrow.

See, you get it beaten into you pretty early on that good soldiering is basically all about being able to look after yourself better than the other guy. Being able to admin yourself more effectively so that when the shit hits the fan you're in better shape to fight. And win. And part of that is all the boring stuff. Knowing exactly how much water you've got and how easily you can reach your morphine and which way the ammo link is facing when you're laying it in along the bottom of your daysack so you can feed it straight to the gunner. Like I say, dull in extremis. But necessary.

Ah. That cosy grey area between rigour and superstition.

I think we'd probably prefer to call it professionalism. But point taken. Might make an interesting recruitment campaign to ditch all those cinematic coastal assaults and just run a thirty second ad of a guy trying to dry and talc his feet at three am with Dartmoor blowing one of her trademark hoolies.

I must say that, all things considered, I rather prefer the dinner and cocktail party circuit of the service.

You might be onto something there.

And are you all set for our little talk?

Absolutely.

Good. Here's the deal. Our man, Abdul Mahmood Khan Achakzai, was the de facto Governor of Gereshk until the invasion in 2001. Since then he's been one of Karzai's Durrani cronies on the senate. The word from my team in Kabul is that Achakzai's a sharp customer and he doesn't suffer fools gladly. So we don't want to bullshit him. Speak frankly and positively. As I said to you earlier you won't need to engage with him much, but you do need to be prepared to discuss the general strategy in terms that will paint the Brigadier in a favourable light. Do we have an understanding?

I thought this wasn't going to be a *political tête-à-tête*, sir?

It doesn't hurt to be prepared, that's all. And I have an uncomfortable feeling that he'll be more interested in what you have to say than in anything we have to bring to the table.

I wet my lips.

Oh, and one other thing to consider. Achakzai's newest wife is fourteen. All perfectly legal of course, if a bit on the grubby side considering the forty-year age gap, but certainly not the progressive that our deskbound friends back in the UK were hoping for. So besides being a tricky little shit, our new governor is also technically a paedophile. – Laughing, wagging a finger at me – One day, when I write my memoirs, I'll have to include some sort of a foreword at the start of this particular chapter to clarify that nothing contained therein is in any way a distortion of the truth, lest it be mistaken for a heavy-handed attempt at satire. Working with the Afghans *can* be frightfully surreal. So. Which vehicle would you like me in?

Jacko arranged them out front of the wagons, waving them in

at the edges until he had them squarely framed and foregrounded, the Hesco spiral-wire backdrop sitting level for the shot. It was a ritual thing they had. They struck a scruffy spread of war poses and bulldog flexing and these put-on pouts of indifference and put-on pouts of boredom and white grins on tan skin and bonnet-sprawled ankle-exposing seductions and semi-covert offensive hand gestures. I stepped up to take the picture. Say *jihad*. Two of them were caught mid-blink, the rest with their faces screwed partially against the glare.

That's your lot. Let's get this show on the road.

They lined up and loaded their weapons and made them ready into the sandbags against the far wall. The familiar crunch of the working parts snapping into place. I squeezed myself into the passenger seat of the second vehicle and stood my rifle barrel-down between my knees and smoothed out a laminated map of the city on my legs. My body armour and weapons pouches had me wedged in a rigid upright position with my helmet jammed in against the roof of the cabin. Woody climbed into the driver's seat and flicked the ignition. The convoy choked into life. A guard at the front gate gave us the thumbs up and I signalled to the lead vehicle to move out. The two gates were unbolted and pulled open. Ahead of us the low horizon shimmered and boiled.

(sapphire zero this is sapphire three moving out to checkpoint one over)

I watched Bennett on top cover on the lead vehicle swing his gun in a slow arc left-to-right-to-left as the convoy pushed out in single file across the open stretch of scrubland ringing the base. At the north end we could see contractors huddled flat to a wall in a slip of shade and irregular rows of fuel tankers painted out in diesel-greased reds and greens, their truck cabins flashing with baubles and beaded strings and flags and blinking lights and lurid corporate motifs. Blended with the grunt of exhaust fumes and horns sounding off there was something about the procession that resembled the pomp and grotesquery of a circus parade.

We cut a hard left and swung west towards the market place, children in dirtbleached shalwar kameez chafing the convoy in short sprints (hey! hey mister! hey! salaam alaikum! hey!), the men tilling the small fields at the outskirts glancing up and then returning to their work. Behind us a plumed wall of white dust and the sun high up overhead where the sky had been scrubbed clean by the storm. A single white cloud brush-stroked against the aching blueness.

We came off the track onto the tarmac road with the market bursting into life either side of us. We drove quickly. There were many small dark shops that opened out onto the road and men working at the stalls set out at the roadside and children splashing in the wastewater trenches. You could hear the tinny blast of Punjabi pop music playing out from wind-up radios, the songs warbling and stretching and bending out of shape as we passed. Old men gathered on the street corners stared at us in silence, unmoving, shisha smoke creeping up in blue curls over painted beards and painted eyes. There were pink sunhardened bodies of goat and lamb strung up in rows underneath plastic canopies and the naan smoke sizzling off open ovens caught the sunlight in long, dusty slats. And everywhere that crazy beautiful perfume of burning charcoal and body odour and marijuana seeping through the vehicle air-con in lukewarm gasps.

Up front Bennett was waving oncoming traffic to the sides of the road as we bellowed through. I counted three white Toyotas.

(sapphire zero this is three approaching checkpoint one over moving through to target location over)

I folded my map away as we turned off along a one-lane dirt

track that dipped and potted between a ragged cascade of shanty houses spilling off from the main concourse, all corrugated iron and sheets of rusty porous tin and the walls plastered with pieces of straw and chicken wire and magazine pull-outs that jutted out of the packed earth like nubbed bonework. Clotheslines hung up over the track clipped past overhead forcing Bennett to drop inside the cabin. Our tyres running up a frothy tidemark of rank brown water against the walls. Next to me Woody whistling A Life on the Ocean Wave.

At the end of the track we turned eastwards onto Route Bravo on the approach to the political quarter and the governor's compound, swapping the casual disorder of the slums for gated residential estates fitted out in polished marble and banks of sunblazed turquoise glass.

Hey Woody. Any idea how you're supposed to address a provincial governor?

Not a clue boss. – Thinking this over – Although if I'm the one talking to the governor then I think we can assume the shit has really hit the fan.

I quickly ran through a mental checklist of the etiquette we'd been schooled during operational training: keep the soles of your boots covered; avoid touching food or people with your left hand; accept all offers of hospitality; a handshake and a hand on the heart for greeting; never acknowledge the women; enquire about their health and their families. I couldn't remember ever going over the minutiae of making small talk with a middle-aged man who has recently married a child.

I saw the compound coming into view and there was that familiar pulse of adrenaline running right to the tips of my fingers.

(sapphire zero this is sapphire three approaching target location now over)

The lead vehicle slowed as we reached the barrier at the entrance. The convoy came to a halt.

Fucking guard's asleep boss, the voice coming in over my headset.

Jacko mashed his horn three times and I watched the guard spill backwards off his chair in the pillbox. Our vehicles hummed.

In my wing mirror I saw two little girls skip across from a market stall towards the rear vehicle, arms and fingers outstretched to Tait on top cover *pleasepleaseplease*, Tait leaning down to toss them a confetti of boiled sweets and stickers and pens.

From behind them, a figure stepped out of the stall and out of the shadows and in two strides was up against the vehicle up between the children and –

a fucking bang and then a blast of air like a fist to the back of my head that smashes my face on the dashboard and I black out for a second and when I come to my ears are ringing and black smoke is churning around our vehicle and someone is screaming CONTACT on the net and I can hear the pitterpatter of soft things splashing out of the sky.

I scramble out of my vehicle. My wing mirror is gone. This smell of burning plastic, something else too. The ground is scorched. Bonzo rushes up to me out of the smoke.

They've hit the rear vehicle boss.

I can see the cab burning and I get this hot wash of saliva high in my throat but some part of me shuts down and I hear myself calm and firm and abrupt even though I think I might have pissed myself.

I want the lads in a perimeter around the convoy. Now. Seal off the road at both ends. And get those two VIPs inside the compound right away.

(sapphire zero this is sapphire three contact wait out)

Everywhere there is movement and noise.

Two marines and the medic drag Tait from the burning vehicle. The blast has taken off his lower jaw and his arms and most of his face and scalp. The medic opens his throat in two quick cuts and slides in a red pipe to get him breathing and he's saying come on mate, hang in there, it's ok, over and over and he's pumping his ribs with his hands clasped, forearms red to the elbow, one-and-two-and-three-and-four and I stand there useless and it's only when one of the marines has to pull the medic off that I realise Tait is dead.

(sapphire zero we have at least one man T4 and two children T4 looks like a suicide attack we need a QRT and a medevac helicopter at the target right now right away)

Sirens somewhere in the distance. People gathered at the edges of the roadblock. Women screaming. Police and security contractors scatter out of the compound. They start pushing the crowds back with the butts of their rifles. Jacko and another marine have secured the road fifty yards south of our position and the patrol is now exposed along a narrow stretch of tarmac. From where I'm standing I can see the rear vehicle sucked in on itself and crumpled and pockmarked all over with puncture holes from one-inch ball bearings. Smoke coming out in thick clouds from under the wheel arches, flecks of fat and skin splashed out across the side of the cabin. I'm suddenly alert to the possibility of another bomber detonating amongst the crowd.

Hamid. – Gesturing to the terp squatted by the main gate – Hamid I need the police to move those people back and hold the end of the road while we bring the other vehicles into the compound. This is very important. Do you understand?

He doesn't move.

I said do you understand?

He turns and catches my eye and then nods.

The three front vehicles are driven inside the compound. One of the marines grenades the bombed vehicle to take out anything that can't be left behind. The rear cabin burns and flares and dies in a white phosphorous soap.

I'm so buzzed up on adrenaline that I can't tell if it has been seconds or minutes since the attack and when I stop to catch myself time suddenly seems to crash into a slow drag around me and I'm watching it all happen with my arms banging uselessly against my sides, everything floating out of time in a lazy underwater waltz: someone is shouting do we have any walking wounded; Woody and another drag Tait's body in behind the barrier on a sheet of tarpaulin, marking out a long dirty umbilical stain that snakes all the way back to where the wagon is cooking on its chassis; they wrap Tait in the sheet and I watch them go back out and begin carefully, ohfuck ohfuck ohfuck, *reverentially*, picking up what's left and placing it into a plastic bin liner. I look right and Jonas is standing quietly to one side staring down at the trail in the dirt and it seems like he's almost swaying on the balls of his feet even though he is stood stiff and still, his bottom jaw slightly open, and Bonzo walks up to him slowly and takes him by the shoulders and sits him down at the kerbside and he undoes the sweat rag around his neck and he begins smoothing the gore from around his eyes and mouth and nostrils and he spits on the rag to wipe clean skin-coloured spots across his face. Bonzo takes a cigarette from his shirt pocket, lights it, takes a deep drag and then he puts it between Jonas's lips. He brushes the hair off his forehead and pats him twice on the cheek and there is more humanity and compassion in that gesture than anything I have ever seen.

Time races back at me. Colour. Someone is shouting my name.

Hamid sends out eight police to hold the line at the south end and I pull Jacko's fire team inside the compound. They take positions behind sandbags looking out over the sights of their rifles. They're breathing heavy and looking to each end of the roadblock and the way the lids are peeled right back off their eyeballs makes them look hunted and animal. Somewhere close by the throbbing klaxon of a car alarm going off feels like a fist opening and closing deep inside my brain.

(sapphire zero we have established a perimeter inside the target location over what is your status over)

Inside Thornton is slumped with his head between his knees and he keeps looking up and rubbing the back of his neck and stretching off his jaw and eyebrows like he's just taken a hook to the face and then dropping his head back between his knees with a shake. And in that moment I hate him like he's personally responsible for what happened to Tait and I hate him like I want him to be dead too, and it's not until much later that I'm ashamed of my hatred and in its place I only feel a kind of soft and shadowed sadness. An absence of something.

Bonzo, head count mate.

All here and accounted for. Jonas took some shrapnel in the hit but he's in one piece otherwise. Harry can't hear anything. He was in the passenger side when it went off. The medic's looking fucked. But I think that's only from trying to patch Tait up.

Christ.

One of the policemen is pointing and laughing and clutching the sides of his belly and I look up at the roof of the compound and a cat is chewing and hacking at this black stump and it takes me a moment to realise that I'm looking at the head of the bomber with the face scraped off like a worn tyre and two startled pus-coloured eyes staring out and that's the point where my body finally gives in and I lean into my knees and start retching.

(sapphire three this is sapphire zero we have a team approaching your position stand by for extraction out)

the question they always ask, right after the whole did you kill anyone thing, after you've swallowed down the disgust that comes up like bile and that sadness or aloneness that is there often with it, after that they nearly always ask were you scared? and I think to myself (and I'll never say a word of it) scared? you think you want to know what I know about fear? (and I'll never tell them a word of it, not a fucking whisper) about how it got all of us one way or another; about how we got it in a way that was unique to each man alone and in a way that was somehow also seeded with the universal, how it was a lonely thing and a shared thing of the ages, and how this was a mystery and contained within it perhaps were the answers to many of the unanswerable things of living; and about how it didn't get us cold or sudden but that it came to us in warmth and rapprochment, like something once intimate but long forgotten, something rehearsed, dearly awaited, and how in this way it was no different to love or bravery or death and how our lives until that moment had been a magnificence of small fears and small braveries and small passions and small deaths, and how, like those other grand and long wished-for moments, when it finally came upon us in fullness we showed not surprise not bitterness but said only to ourselves: oh, I have been here before, I knew this all along; and about how it was as though finding ourselves obscured in a great forest we had stumbled across our own footprints right there in the dirt, arriving at a place we had never visited before and knowing it for the hundredth time; and about how, without ever articulating as much to ourselves, we came to feel we would never live an honest and revelatory moment in our lives, that the fear was only buff and shine over the gathered offcuts of the past, fragments of living and dreaming and story and youth, that we had already lived our greatest moments in increments and in tablecrumbs; eternal recurrence in a single life; but when they ask it of me, all shiny-eyed and dimple-cheeked in anticipation of some cheap kick, I'll offer them up instead some bland

21

and meagre platitude to make them dismiss, in a covert roll of the eyes,
every small thing I hold dear – and I'll never tell, not ever

H-8

It was the night before the start of the campaign. Reconnaissance patrols had been bumping the enemy lines outside the town for forty-eight hours. The main assault companies were poised and offset and attending to their final preparations and all night they heard the low chudder of helicopters parsing back and forth the thick and starless sky. Many weeks of planning and manoeuvres and logistics preceded this moment. A senior leader from the town had defected in advance of the fighting.

The men from Lima Company had received their orders for the operation against the fort early in the evening and Major Palmer had told them that not all of them would be coming home but that they would face the enemy with ferocity and cunning and loyalty to one another. The speech had the must of a thing much revised. Afterwards they made carbonara in empty ammunition tins from dried pasta and blocks of canned cheese and slivers of fried spam and eating it, grinning at each other over the stunt blue flames of the stoves, they felt obscene and grandiose and kingly as only those without can ever know in fullness. Then they were left to the dark and the insides of their heads and the fear came as in the onset of a summer storm and the only generality that can be claimed was that each of them sought it in the eyes of another and each saw only a counterfeit of his own horror mirrored back at him.

JB watched Buck where he lay cornerwise against the brickwork, his face in flickering darkness and the folds of the sleeping bag pulled up high over his shoulders. A thin membrane of chalk downing his hair and hands and shape so that the very edges of him seemed to leach into the darkness. He didn't look to breathe. To JB sleep seemed a kindness too far, something to be rationed and shared and not gorged upon by those it deigned to visit. He turned back to where his equipment was laid out in regular, obnoxious rows on the concrete. He blew out his cheeks. It put him in mind of when he had competed at county level: the careful days of preparation prior to a race where he would fine-tune his diet to an accuracy of individual calories, would taper his training regime to match clinical data specifying distance and time right to the nearest minute. How he would change the laces on his training shoes the night before, just in case, just in case. And the object of all this was to surmount chance's role in the play of things, to build himself a levee against the dice roll of the gods. It was a comfort and a crutch and it made him ball up inside to see his secrets fashioned so crudely on the flooring before him.

JB inspected each object individually and he blew the dust from it and packed it into his webbing and daysack and pockets according to a sequence honed through fierce selective pressures, and he tested the looseness of his webbing against his shoulders and kidneys and he taped the excess straps flush to the yolk. He chewed the tail of his pen and walked himself through each of the waypoints on the map: the hill off to his flank at the first, the valley floor dropping away to his right; perhaps a glint of the river mirrored up moonlit from its hollowed traverse; at the second, the long flat battlement of the fort itself, the enemy bunkers mounted at the corners. Trip flares and machine gun placements and killing zones. Only when he had assured himself of acquitting his responsibilities before fate was he able to give himself up to the partiality of what was to follow, to the sleep that eluded him like a rumour half unheard.

He took a deep breath, threw his legs out. Somewhere far off there was a deep and silent jackhammer booming that he felt puddle through him. There is a picture of him from that night, long lost now, and in that picture he is leaning back into a canvas stool with his machine gun across his lap and ribbons of seven-six-two brass hefted over one shoulder. He had reckoned to strike a warrior's pose. But the picture is unflattering in the clarity of its recollection and what it shows is a face paling into translucence; features soft and neutered to the dilutions of the flash, pinspot pupils swum in white and vivid eyes sunk into the blueshadowed bowl of his sockets; a gaze that looks into the lens and through it and beyond; a gaze venturing out into unfathomed and disconsolate places.

At the other side of the pen Cheeks was sitting with his bag pulled up under his armpits and his knees drawn against his chest. He had a spiral bound notebook open against his legs. The light from his head torch swung the solid shadowed relief of the room into disarray.

Hey. Watcha doing?

Nothing much. He didn't look up. He had his bottom lip stuck out as he wrote, the tip of his tongue wetting it side to side.

Go on. Tell me.

He looked off. Writing my last letter home. You know. Just in case.

Bit late in the day for that sort of thing, isn't it?

Not for me. I've written a ton of them already.

Pause.

I don't get it.

I've kind of started making a habit of it. Writing a new last letter before we've got a big fight lined up. Must have written fifteen or twenty by now.

How come?

You ever try writing one?

No.

It's fucking hard, that's how come.

Pause

I remember trying to write my first before we even flew out. It seemed like the sensible thing to do. But that was awful. God awful.

Yeah?

Oh yeah. – Laughing – The first one just ended up like this big self-pity wank fest. Like if you've ever tried imagining your own funeral. Like you're trying to write this letter that will be meaningful for your missus and your kids and the friends you're leaving behind and all that, except that really it's all about you you you. It was bullshit. Embarrassing.

So then what?

So then I wrote another. A few days after we flew in. This one was loads better. A bit cooler. A bit more detached, if you get what I mean. Yeah, that wouldn't have been a bad one to get delivered if it came to it. Cold and funny and like, yeah, being dead's shitty and all but life goes on so don't be sad for me etcetera etcetera. That kind of thing. The perspective was better on that one. Not perfect, but better than the first.

He thumbed out a scruff of tobacco onto liquorice rolling paper and piped it out into a cigarette tight and point and he lit it and took a deep lungful and sank back into his bergen and he stared out into the night and after a moment he let go a long thin bud of smoke that shone and clouded theatrically in the wash of the torch.

But then we got onto those first big patrols. Back in early October. Remember the shootout by Harlequin Point? About then. And I got to thinking that the second letter was a bit too cold like. It needed a bit more humour in there, a bit more spark. So I wrote another. And then another. And it was like every one I wrote went too far one way or the other. Too cold or too funny or too self-pitying or too clever, but that each time I drafted one I was getting just that little bit closer to the ideal. You know what I mean?

No.

I kind of enjoy it now. It's part of the routine. It helps me clear my head. You know, putting pen to paper and banging out a quick five or six or seven hundred words. I'd recommend it. Have you got one writ?

Me? No.

You thought about it?

No. Sounds kinda gay to me.

JB didn't say it but he had lately come to the conclusion that he had put off writing such a letter for too long now, that his reticence had assumed a talismanic quality of itself.

Huh. – Cheeks taking another couple of drags and blowing his smoke up at the patchwork plastering and watching it moulder and dissipate – You hear about that bootneck that left a fully paid-up trip to Vegas for friends and family in his will? That's something else, don't you think? I mean, you've got to be thinking pretty far ahead to come up with something like that. I guess this is similar. In its own way. It's like, if things go wrong for me, no one can ever say I didn't see it coming. No one can ever say I got blindsided. The evidence is all there. I've been prepping for it hard.

You shouldn't talk that way. It's not right.

It don't matter how we talk, not really.

Well it matters to me.

Ok.

Pause.

So. You all ready for tomorrow?

Ready as I'll ever be.

Yeah. Me too.

JB lay there in his bag with his eyes squeezed shut and he practised every trick he knew to bring sleep in and his head rattled with amphetamine thoughts that blatted and ricocheted and he humped onto his left and then onto his right and after a time he lay out on his back with his hands under his head watching clouds of wet breath form and unform over his face. Sleep never came.

At two o'clock he started waking the others. Stand to, lads. Stand to.

D DAY

There was the long, sick-making infiltration by Viking where each of them made silent promises to themselves in a way that was not wholly dissimilar to prayer. At H-Hour the first Viking broke the frontline of enemy forces and the dark went bright in a winter of gunfire and explosions that concussed right through their bellies. The marines were taking effective fire, military parlance for being very deep in the shit. Bullets flaying helmet covers and punching clean holes through consecutive pouches on their webbing. JB caught a nice one through the bunching of his jacket. Major Palmer refused to step outside his Viking at the command position and sought to direct the attack from the guts of the vehicle. They were forced into a retreat against a heavy weight of direct fire and four marines were lifted from the emergency RV with gunshot wounds running from scuffed skin and muscle to fist-sized exit wounds blown open against ripstock and Kevlar plating. In the morning Palmer was relieved of his post and flown back to the UK and there was a sense of scandal swiftly ground out by the arrival of the new Major who marked his territory in quick and thunderous and rhetoric-heavy passes up and down the company lines.

H+12

They sat out at the harbour location with the new day turning the near horizon into boiling glass and the cleansing smell of gunsmoke on their skin and clothes and they chainsmoked and affected a swagger and a bravado they had not felt at the time but now recalled in almost-sincerity. Two of the Viking drivers were sat in the open rear cabin doors passing a smoke. One of them was working a khaki pleat down off each thigh and Cheeks called over and said, watcha doing there Taff? and the driver looked down at his legs and then up again and said, these? aw these are just tourniquets the medic borrowed me. These fuckers have a habit of blowing your legs off if you hit an IED. – Banging the side of the vehicle lovingly with an open palm – We've had it happen three times in the last two months. See, if we drive with the tourniquets on we can fasten them nice and tight soon as we get hit. Save us bleeding out. And Cheeks nodded and turned back to the others, quite satisfied with this explanation, and it is not something he thinks of again until his wedding night several months later when, half cut, he watches his new wife unfastening her garter and he is suddenly back in the desert and it is nightime and he is prostrate atop a quivering, spurting mountain of severed limbs that hum with an obscenity of old raw pork, and later, much later, the doctor will describe visual hallucinations as being *a positive psychotic symptom* – a pause, a smile – *treatable*.

There had been hard fighting through the night and into the morning and they could hear it whispered and percussive still on the corners of the wind. The enemy was well dug-in at the frontiers of the town. In the south the Afghan Kandaks had made only creeping progress against the gun nests and mobile sniper teams, and further north the British and American deliberate company attacks had been hobbled by minefields sown irregular and unmarked. Three coalition soldiers had died before sunrise.

Lima Company's failure to seize the fort was fed up and down the chain as a tactical withdrawal, the words conferring an element of deliberation and foresight unapparent in the ugly horror of the night. They sat and they watched packets of supplies cutting fresh trails towards them across the desert floor and they studied the charge and concentration of the troop commanders hurrying between vehicles, and they divined in it all an urgency and a weight of expectation that burned off any last hopes of reprieve. The message came through soon enough: they were to take the fort at dawn the next morning. The phrase *whatever the cost* never spoken but sitting underneath everything, echoing up through half-heard phrases and euphemism. The entire operation to capture the town, men, the new Major explained in patient, resolute tones, lies with this success.

Buck and JB saw the dusk in from the sentry position overlooking the road junction and the footbridge crossing the leat. They were running a hard routine: by nightfall it was two hours at the post followed by one hour's sleep hot-bagging one of the slugs. Buck always said it was the worst of the war. He thought that was funny. The ground was flat and the sky clear and the night came in swift and granular and it turned the familiar points on the foreground blue and liquid and untrue. The fear grew with the dark and settled like sediment in the lonely hollowed places of them.

Hey, Buck?

Yeah.

I was thinking. About what happened.

Yeah.

What do you reckon made the boss freak out like that?

Well I'm guessing the shooting and the explosions might have done their bit.

I mean, why him? Why then?

Pause.

You want to know what I think? I think when it comes down to it he was just plain cold pussy and that's all there is. There ain't nothing else to it worth killing yourself over.

Yeah, maybe. I don't know. Thing that gets me is that every REMF in theatre will be saying exactly the same. About him being a pussy. You know, while they're stacking blankets or pushing papers or cooking up breakfast or whatever. What the fuck would they know about it? About any of it?

JB was looking out in a hard stare over his rifle.

There's that quote about the guy in the arena. I can't remember who said it. Something about sweat and blood and dust, and about failing while aiming high. Do you know the one I mean? Like it's better to have come up short than to just stand there passing judgement from the sidelines. Maybe it could have just as easily been any of us, maybe we were lucky. Maybe that's the way it works. I don't know.

He looked back at Buck.

Well. That's what gets me about it anyway. It just leaves a dirty taste.

Like I said, it ain't nothing worth killing yourself over – Buck hauling the conversation up short, suspicious of it swerving without forecast into thickets and longgrass. All these green college and university kids coming up through the ranks with their heads stuff-filled to bursting with big words and big thoughts and none of it meaning a fucking thing of use.

Here, pass me those.

Buck turned onto one side and grabbed the night vision goggles and ran a quick figure-eight over the junction and then up the road and then east to west along the horizon, just like they had been taught in training. Not the tightest fitting jonny in the pack: that's what the others said about him. Mostly to his face, which was ok. But no one could say shit about his soldiering. He had the soldiering all wrapped up, sweet as a nut. It was a point of pride.

He made one more diligent sweep with the goggles. Hot dust green buzzed his eyes and when he lowered them again the night was a thick and liquid black.

What do you think about going back in?

Pause.

Not much.

Pause.

Me neither.

What time is it?

Eleven fifteen.

Christ.

At five to twelve JB gave Cheeks a shake and at two minutes past Cheeks slowdragged his helmet and rifle up onto the point and slumped next to Buck and muttered something and stuck out his rifle. Buck watched back over his shoulder as JB shook himself into the bag and rolled his jacket under his head. He turned out again.

A night wind was sounding off the plains a bottleblown note that made the settled sediment feeling down inside him stir an uneasy pattern. Black shapes on black seemed to jump and shift until he held them just off-centre in his vision where they fixed themselves, suddenly innocent and stolid. The night was all lies and it tried to break a man's resolve with its sleights and nudges and being this far behind enemy lines it seemed to animate the stillness into unprecedented vigour. He put the goggles to his eyes and the rocks and the junction calmly buzzed the night vision and the balding grass blew and there was nothing else.

Buck looked again over his shoulder to where he could make out JB wrapping his fingers silently against the lining of the bag, staring up blindly into the sky. It made Buck pissed to see it. As a recruit he had learned the peculiar terror that the prospect of no sleep induced in him, and he had become artful in thieving minutes of quick shuteye in the least welcoming of places. Every reclaimed moment of unconsciousness at the back of a coach or a wagon, mid-lecture, in the shower even, another kick against the pricks. He had noticed in himself what the fighting had done to this sturdy old part of him. How the sleep had become uncertain and anxious and light, like a coat of fine rain out in the sun. And how this change seemed to portend deeper aberrations out of sight right in the workings of him. A tightening all the way down so that you could never tell when the whole thing might threaten to snap off its axle and tear at everything else inside. What did JB think he was doing? Why wasn't he sleeping while he had the chance? What did he have to think about that was so important? Didn't he know all this nervousness was catching and it was ruining everyone else's sleep? Who the fuck did he think he was?

He shook his head at the outrage of it all.

Half past midnight and out beyond the junction there was the faint bellsound of cattle. The gentle chiming looked to blow up from the combing grass, so light of touch was the noise, so near and so hidden. It had a sinister remembrance to it. Buck imagined a boy goatherd, half-asleep himself, driving his train along the road under fatted and heavylidded eyes, slapping absently with a leather crop at the ankles, not knowing that even then his every step was overseen by men dressed in shadows who watched his passage over sighted weapons, the shorn bowl of his head bobbing slumbered along a faultline marked by the noiseless whistle of rifle muzzles where two bullets were primped and readied to fly. It was a bad thought, a bad unwholesome thought, and it whipped up the fear all the way down in him again. He felt it racing his veins as though suddenly loosed after long days of abstinent bravado; felt the exposure of their position out there on the point like a keen chill riding his back, creeping long-fingered at the places not warmed by his own quickening eyes; felt the presence of evil men gathering there in the lapping darkness, encircling them and capturing them and opening their throats where they lay, and the chiming of grazing animals nearby rocked itself lightly on the lullaby breeze, and he thought of a boy goatherd leading them ever onwards into the darkness and he thought of two and then five and then ten and then fifty goatherds swinging in a devil circle a ring a ring a roses and each of them wearing the boy's face, two clean bullet holes puncturing each forehead as a judgement upon him, a judgement upon them all, and the goatherds laughing and splashing knee-deep in arterial blood and animal milk that warmed and heaved and roiled and the chime the chime the chime –

The hit was clean, driving the helmet down through his face so his chin and teeth clattered on the cheekpiece of his rifle.

What the fuck? A hot wet whisper into one ear.

Buck mumbled something irate and half-formed out of his funk.

Were you asleep? What the fuck? – Cheeks batting him again on the helmet – Wake the fuck up.

I'm sorry, I –

Do I have to keep you up myself? Like, do you actually require me to read you a story or some shit to keep you useful? Can I get you an espresso? We're out here in the middle of fucking nowhere with these bum bandits crawling all over the place and *now's* the time you start catching up on your beauty sleep? – Pause – Buck, you arsehole.

Buck shook his jaw and blinked hard and took up the goggles again. All the fear and fatigue dropped out of him in quick release.

Do it again and I'll fucking shoot you myself.

Buck sneered to himself, indignant, and set to a quick figure-eight out where a small trudge of goats was herding the junction and then up along the road and east to west across the horizon. He hadn't even been asleep, had only rested his eyes for a moment. That's all. There wasn't no one could say shit about his soldiering. It was a point of pride.

D+1 AND D+2

Lima took the fort in the early hours, the new Major turreted in his Viking at the spearhead of the charge. The kind of gesture to earn a man accusations of being a medal chaser and a risk taker and a hero. They pressed on through to the far eastern edge of the town. The rain set in hard by late that morning. The fighting turned dirty and amateurish and a confused stalemate was established and the day drew on with the reports of rocket fire and grenades damped by soft fields and a grey and scanty and sidelong rain. There was word there had been successful breakthroughs to the north and south. By nightfall the marines watched, grateful and disgusted, as a column of D Squadron Scimitars and Jackals forded the temporary lines and made entry into the town. The fighting was over in a rush. Afterwards they patrolled the deserted town. Fires left in haste still smoked and hissed; coalition airdrop leaflets pulped like porridge oats underfoot. A light rain was falling and a low dawn mist rattled over the debris and soldiers from one of the Afghan Kandaks hoisted the flag over the empty streets at midday to distant media fanfare and the applause of officialdom and a bored-looking contortion of sky.

D+3

Lima sent out reassurance patrols into the town centre in the aftermath hours where there was no one left to reassure but the wild dogs that noted their paths through rainblack rubble and small, resolute spikes of fire and the grey unwash of a morning that never fully broke. The threat from booby traps kept them to the open streets like beggars. They walked the roads with their shoulders turned down and their boots dragging, the fuckrush of the fight already in withdrawal and a baggy, sodden tiredness settling over them.

They sat up in the police station and attended to themselves and kicked their legs carelessly from the open scaffolded floors. Notice came that the general himself was expected to oversee the formal handover to the Afghans. An advance party arrived and made turning circles in the lot outside the station and a small, clean, eagle-faced lieutenant prowled the company making faces at loose piles of grenades and peat-black combats stripped to dry and other sign of the fighting, and he spun on his toes when he came to where Buck was quartered atop an emptied mortar tin, asking why he hadn't thought it necessary to fucking shave Corporal Rogers and if he thought he might be above the fucking rules or if maybe he was just plain fucking lazy. Old man Buck had a clear ten years and fifty pounds on the stripling and in his face there was still that savage, ugly slackness that the fighting imparted to them all by degree, and JB and Cheeks and others from the troop stared on light-headed with a residual bloodlust percolating through them as Buck wearied to his feet, faced down the lieutenant, shook his head once, violently, and said, quite simply, quite quietly: yes. Sorry sir. (It had all the hallmarks of a classic dit in the making but it left an unaccountable sorriness behind it, and afterwards that sorriness seemed to also assume whatever guilt or disgust was felt over the fighting. The incident was not referred to again).

Cheeks sat close over the stove and stirred the old tin mug with the old tin spoon. He watched the stewing greyscale food turn itself over against the rim of the mug. Steam woke the cracks on windbitten fingers. He dipped into his webbing and pulled out a stack of banded papers that he placed properly to one side. Beneath was a threadworn canvas wash bag that he unrolled neat and precise next to where he sat. He rubbed his hands. From the first pocket he produced a quarter-sized bottle of chilli sauce that he unscrewed and splashed into the mug. He gave the food a stir and the chilli hit his nostrils. He plucked two spice jars wrapped tight in layers of harry black to prevent them from shattering, one with *mixed herbs* written in permanent marker beneath the lid, the other annotated *garlic salt*. He eyed both in parallel and decided on the mixed herbs and he scattered a fingerpinch into the mix. Another stir. It was shaping up to be a fine pot mess and he congratulated himself on his discipline and foresight. There was that old saying about laziness and discipline: *any fool can be uncomfortable in the field*. But in Cheeks' estimation it took a real somebody to rustle up such a class act out of the bland carby slops and slaw rationed out at them in bulk. It was testament to a certain kind of character. It said something. Especially after everything that had happened.

Here, JB. Give this a taste. JB leaned in and cupped the spoon with one hand.

Shit. That's some good stuff you got there. Not bad at all.

Cheeks gave the serious nod of a master craftsman.

What's in it?

If I told you, I'd have to kill you.

Right.

A cold rain was blowing up from the open courtyard and his feet were like hams against the ends of his boots. He lifted the mug and blew the spoon and tasted it and studied it and added a final measured splash of chilli.

He pointed over at the fraying double-punch of the bullet hole on JB's sleeve.

Quite the souvenir.

Yeah.

Could do with getting me one of those. What do you do? Just stand side-on and shuffle towards the firing point?

JB smiled. Yeah. Something like that.

Cheeks presented a tube of cream cheese from out of the wash bag and JB returned a single nod of admiration. Cream cheese was a big deal if you could get your hands on it. During the summer months, when its shelf life ran for days rather than weeks, a decent tube might have commanded two or three packs of cigarettes in the field. Cheeks squeezed it out over the mess and it leant an immediate colour to the red-brown watery strains. An unctuous greasy luxury. This act afforded him a deep and simple satisfaction.

You know I was thinking of ditching it. The jacket.

Bollocks you were.

I'm serious. It's not something I really want reminding of all the time. Having it sitting there on my arm. Got the wind picking through it day and night. It's like maybe I used up all of my bad luck or all of my good luck in one go only I'm not sure which. And I'm not too keen to find out either.

Cheeks fixed him suspiciously. He felt a little wrong-footed.

Really?

Yeah.

Pause.

Huh. – Shrugging – Shit, if I was you I'd have that fucker framed and halfway shipped home already.

You can have it. It's yours.

Don't be stupid. What would I want with your jacket anyway? It was stupid talk. It made him feel cheated somehow just to entertain it. All this good luck bad luck bullshit.

A film of steam peeled up the length of the warming spoon. Cheeks lifted it clear and the food spilled off in a thin clear sauce. He broke over the mug two biscuit browns that he crumbled to powder and worked in deep until the pot mess thickened to paste, the spoon handle stood bolted to attention at the centre of the mug. He stirred it once more and tasted it. His hands were working an obedient charade but his thinking felt nudged gently out of joint. It was something in what JB had said. Something he couldn't quite place.

The mug bubbled up to spits on the stove and he ran the spoon through it and he could feel the mess inside good and thick and cooked through to a fleshy soft. He flicked the flame on the stove and sat off the sweating steaming mug to cool and he sidled back and crossed his boots at the ankles and JB gestured over to him *bon appétit*. The world never looked quite so mean with clean feet and fresh socks and a pot of hot food stewing away beside you. He promised himself again that he would never take a hot meal for granted in his whole fucking life.

Cheeks gave it as long as seemed decent, his mouth wet and warm in anticipation, and the first spoonful gummed his palate in an immediate stubborn napalm clump. JB laughing as he hot-breathed the worst of it down his chin and shirt.

He ate, open-mouthed, breathing steam.

Good?

Good. – A mess of teeth and tongue and food – You want some?

JB shook his head.

Down in the courtyard there was a shudder of movement and voices and one of the troop commanders, his cheeks drawn with tiredness and thirst and stubblegrain dirt, cleaned his kit onto one arm and sounded a two-minute warning down the line for the general's arrival.

Fuck's sake, said Cheeks, glancing down at the near-full mug.

Always the way of it mate.

Cheeks considered this and shrugged it off in a glance and he set himself about the mug again with quick determined spoonfuls.

He chewed his food over, his legs bolted out stubbornly in front of him, watching the troop as they busied their kit. He chewed his food over and he puzzled on the question of the jacket. It troubled him with a quiet insistence. What would make you want to throw something like that away? In a way he couldn't explain or justify there was the rank aftertaste to it of an accusation left without redress. He remembered how it had been at the end of the fighting: tromping the after-storm with the mud mulching cold and gritty in his boots and his nuts froze up inside like stones and his body hair all fuzzed on end, marking slow progress by the little spots of townfire pipped out along a dark and distant buntline. Looking face to face as they marched and swapping swallowed kid grins that you could only really tell from the high pinch of their cheeks and from the way all the thunder had gone out of their shoulders and from a certain cut to the eyes, a refugee stare, blank and disbelieving, a stare common to those unaccustomed to success without great cost. Eyes that gave nothing and, in doing so, also told very much. Into those faces Cheeks had read brazen declarations of how they had done the simplest and the hardest things when it had been required of them: of the hard-on sweetness of victory and of being scared shitless the whole time, and of the two being so closely jointed it wasn't so much a problem of picking them apart, of finding where one ended and the other began, but of saying with any certainty that they weren't, after all, one and the same. And he remembered all this, the windtossed quiet and the wet and the plains and the bonfire smells, and he remembered reading it there plainly in their eyes like what he had thought to be an easy thing understood without explanation.

What would make you want to throw something like that away?

Outside the rain had fallen away to fog and a wetness on the wind that was working itself inside the walls of the station. Below: the booted report of the Afghan honour guard bracing to attention in the courtyard to receive the general's procession.

Cheeks looked up at JB. Looked him direct as though searching for a proof that they had been there together. That they knew the same secrets. About how the fear was all borrowed and playacting and strutting and fretting, and all real all the same. About how it laid waste to everything else of value, how it lent the world clean edges, an ephemeral heroin brilliance that made the very fabric of them thrill in gratitude and wonder. How it turned everything else to deadtime and ruin, and about how it was still the very best of them for all of that. He looked JB direct and purposeful and what he saw was only the reach of distance between them: at once brothers in arms and strangers sundered by the iron lung of those things for which there no words or fit expression. *A lonely thing and a shared thing of the ages.*

Cheeks wrapped and retied and packed the canvas wash bag and he disassembled the gas stove and he rinsed out the tin mug. Left next to him was the packet of tied and sealed and addressed last letters. Cheeks unzipped one of the side pouches on his bergen, a hurried motion, and he stuffed the letters deep under piled and bulging waterproof bags. Like something shameful he didn't calculate on surfacing again.

in the solace and the unrealness of the night, in breath and limb and bloodwarm blindness she says she will never love anyone else, and it is a pitiful touching thing that sincerity alone should almost be sufficient to achieve a truth out of our greatest falsehoods; and we had been back in the city a week or two feeling that maybe we'd had our war already (and we were hell wrong on that) and the lads getting sloppy with their drills the way a drunk undermines his gait to rile up a scuffle of his own clutsyfooted-making, blameless and indignant and righteous; and there was this youngish MFC called patrick that bunked with me who had put a few mortars down the range at musa qala and got this distaste for the fighting that found its expression in curtness and a sort of shrugged contempt for the regalia of mess politics and I liked him a lot for that, and one night I overheard the RSO dripping smiles of conspiratorial poison in the brigadier's ear about that captain Gorman being a hothead and a liability, and afterwards my sacrifice gladdened me like an apology made; and there was that trouble with kilo company, something rumoured and shadowy about two fighting age males getting beaten nearly to death on a night op and the whole thing shut down under a weight of authority and ruthless bureaucratic efficiency and never rightly resolved to our ears and it was difficult not to feel complicit somehow no matter how far out on the peripheries you were: the devil making an abundance to occupy all those idle itchy hands; and I steadied myself at the dining table and I did not look at the RSO and I said sir you'll excuse me if I'm speaking out of turn but in the interests of balance I should say that in my view pat Gorman is an excellent young officer and a credit to his regiment and I stepped away like maybe I had made something right from out of all the wrongness; and some time, she says, to work things out, a bit of space, that's all I need, and I held the phone to my ear for a long time afterward and watched a square of wall that would not draw itself into focus; and I sat out next to pat one evening and we watched the last of the sun and I shook out my cigarettes in a fraternal gesture and he glanced at my offering and then he lifted his face to me, unrecognising, his eyes shimmering with bitterness, and then he looks out again to the sun without uttering so much as a word, as to condemn me, as to cast me down with all the others, to cast me down with himself; see the war made orphans of us and it gathered us up into itself and it was only afterwards, abounded once more by the people we loved, that we would finally realise how alone we were

Jacko and Smudge had been tight for as long as anyone could remember. They didn't gas all that much between themselves but they sat together over breakfast most days and they had got in the habit of crowding out the Six Troop stereo in the early afternoon suntrap, cleaning their rifles and talking shop and play-howling along to old school dance tunes and stripped right down to their knicks so they could bronze off the neat mid-shoulder tidemarks of their soldiers' tans; and on those mornings when patrols were pushed back till late you often found them clearing steady circuits of the perimeter wall, the sun just bleaching up behind long sleeping coils of razor wire. They always seemed to be laughing at someone else's expense: something in the eyes, a knowingness that passed between them in hurried and calculated glances of unstated intent. That made them fuckers to be up against if you were one of the newer guys but useful allies to cultivate and bring onside if you were an old sweat. Spend too much time around them and the whole act got to be a pain. But looking back on things there was a kind of sweetness about it all that you didn't see much of anywhere else back then.

If you watched them hard enough you could sometimes make out the faintest spider of fissures running out under the glossy, solid shell of their alliance. The thing between them was like a carefully weighted set of scales to which they contributed in disproportionate amounts. One always needed more than the other. But the give and take had settled into a careful balance and they had become content with their shares, and that formed the deep-rooted ballast of the thing they had. On those occasions when Smudge was getting ripped on Jacko would almost always manage to snake his way out of frame, a threefold denial, so that he was sided with the baying, good-humoured violence of the crowd, and Smudge would be mad as hell and silent for the evening and in the morning Jacko would pour them both tea into personalised fifty-eight pattern mugs (Jacko's strong with lots of milk, Smudge's strained black and cut with three or four sugars depending on the early start) and this offering would signify a silent truce to all acts of enmity, and by two or three they would be crowded around the speakers again and slicked up in carrot oil and nodding their heads out of time to the chintzy, mechanised punch of a Marshall Jefferson bass line.

They were a fine couple.

It wasn't out of sorts when, in the gym one anonymous Wednesday or Thursday afternoon, they came up with the idea: Jacko asking Smudge what he reckoned the world record for press-ups was, a thousand? Ten thousand? and Smudge, laying himself out on the bench and testing his grip against the barbell, saying, fucked if I know, bet it's a couple more than we need to worry about like, and Jacko chewing it over while he spotted Smudge's lifts, coming out with it abruptly: why don't we train to do a thousand press-ups? and Smudge gently guiding the bar back in to rest on the uprights saying, ok then, yeah, sure, why not?

That was it. Everything else fell into line with a simple kind of inevitability. Word spread. Their boss said bollocks, couldn't be done. Others asked if they were doing it for charity and the chaplain wondered aloud if they were trying to express something about the war, something in allegory perhaps. But they said no, they just wanted to do a thousand press-ups. That was all.

On that first day they sat balled on their knees on a pair of squeaking blue gym mats and they looked over at each other and Jacko said right, let's see what we got. Three whole-body breaths and then a start. Jacko managed forty-eight before his arms buckled; Smudge banged out a swift fifty-nine, the last three showing the strain popping out along his neck. Smudge was swinging his arms out to shake off the burn and showing his teeth as he laughed: remind me whose bright idea this was again?

They gave themselves six weeks. Everything turned to training.

In the mornings they slugged beakers of protein shake before they fell in for orders, the drink turning alternately sludgy and powdery in their mouths no matter how hard they worked it, the sweetener leaving a faint smack of pennycopper on the tongue. They threw out their old training routine and started over, pitching in at the gym in the downtime between patrols or looking to plumb the evening slack before sentry duties began.

The basic circuit consisted of a single set of twenty press-ups: clean, rhythmic, unhurried: the length of the body locked rigid from the neckline right along to the scuffs of their trainers, *all the way up* until the elbows held straight and *all the way down* until the chest was a fist space off the mat: a minute's rest to follow. And repeat. And repeat. And repeat. They would mix in sets with their arms thrown wide in a crucifix to target the chest, or their hands brought in tight under them so their fingers and thumbs formed a diamond on the matting in a way that got the triceps really firing. And it was a marker of the relative tedium of those early sessions to say that this qualified as variety.

On those first days they would wake to tightness across their chests that made it hurt to yawn. A multitude of deep body aches that seemed to finger right inside their bones. They stretched off twice daily and snatched handfuls of ibuprofen before they ate as ritual countermeasure, and in the evenings they would towel-wrap bags of frozen peas to their collars while they lay grumbling and moaning and kicked out on their cots in front of a DVD box set.

Jacko marshalled in weights serials on the off-days for bulk and power and then dropped them again almost as quickly, switching instead to a high-repetition low-weight circuit lovingly wrought over the course of three pencil-chewing patrol briefs and a mine awareness lecture delivered by an itinerant ATO captain. They experimented with plyometric press-ups and knuckle press-ups and Hindu press-ups and Roman press-ups and static press-ups and many variations without name or precedent. They became connoisseurs by necessity, messing with the alchemy of their routine until they achieved a precision instinct for excellence: just the right amount of carbs to keep them working hard off the back-end of a fifty minute conditioning circuit without running up against a sugar crash, or which tracks got them pumped when they needed it (Jacko going in for Bon Jovi; Smudge anything retro hard house), or the way they could change the angle of their elbows in relation to their bodies to squeeze out an extra five when it counted most.

Mid-morning Jacko liked to sit out back of the pods drinking coffee and tossing stones into an emptied peaches-in-syrup ration tin, and he would talk about how it was all a load of bollocks really and how he hated every fucking minute of it, and he would debate the merits and pitfalls of various techniques at length with anyone who cared to pretend to listen.

In that restless in-between time in the early morning, the white tinnitus of an Afghan dawn blushing the edges of the polythene window blinds, blushing their eyelashes, Smudge would dream of the steady, rocking metronome of the movement: the crack of his wrists and elbows as he heaved himself off his elbows on the upwards push, the drop, the sudden relief as he sank again into the lizard compress of the prone position: up and down and up and down and up and down and up and down and – And sometimes when he woke there was that sated emptiness in him that he had known after long nights on operations when it was like his body had turned hollow and dust dry and all the appetite gone from him. Like something vital and life-giving inside had been used up. Those were hard mornings. Jacko often mistook his reticence for laziness and he would jerk between outbursts of barely disguised contempt and hoary old sports clichés that variated loosely on the notion of pain being temporary but pride lasting a lifetime. He sported a t-shirt saying as much.

They checked the weeks off one-by-one on their bespoke EOT deployment calendars. The protein shakes ruined Jacko's guts, something in which he took a certain mucky pride until the day he let a wet one go during the colonel's address to the company. They ran to keep their weight down. In the gym their sets shifted in agonising increments up to twenty-five and then to thirty, the rest time between them dropping to fifty seconds and then to forty-five and then to forty. They trained outside as often as possible, swim shorts rolled high to catch the sun on the top of their thighs, their hands wearing the stigmata of loosely packed gravel grain. The gyms mats blanching in a half moon where their sweat ran onto it.

Training had begun at a pitch of excitement. It quickly swung to boredom and to routine and these were the easiest of days because the boredom spoke of their bodies' gradual adaptation to the strain. Finally the training became habitual, a necessary and comforting component of their daily routine. They got jittery without it.

Jacko had to work hard to keep pace with Smudge's progress, but he was also fired more totally with that complement of bull-headed determination that had seen him win the commando medal as a young recruit. Jacko would stand over Smudge swearing and cajoling as his arms softened to failure and, as Smudge acknowledged secretly to himself at the time (though it was something he would very soon forget), without Jacko there would have been little honest chance of him staying the course. Only once did this dynamic spoil: Smudge telling Jacko to fucking shove his fucking press-ups, flinging the sweat towel across the room before marching out for a long shower where he nursed his bitterness under the hot thin streams until it had fully run out of him. They never spoke of that again and that was an apology of sorts on both sides.

Neither were strangers to bodily punishment or the application of their willpower to great physical feats. There had been the time on the nine-mile speed march four or five years previously when Jacko had shit himself at the exertion, forcing him off to one side as the troop drummed past in a left-right-left-right staccato, flushed with humiliation and disappointment, and one of the training corporals had jogged back to him and said, so what, are you done now? After everything you've put into this? and Jacko had tossed his ruined pants into the hedgerow and sprint-hobbled to rejoin the troop until he was near enough ready to throw chunks down his front (the sign nailed high up in the oak tree: *it's only pain, 500m to go,* the cartoon marine with the polished red cheeks and the outsized combat boots) and at the finish the heavy crotch of his trousers had clung cold to his buttocks and groin and there was this grin writ large on his face that spoke of mastery and wholeness and the ability to do that which should be undoable. In its own way it spoke of transcendence. But something fundamental had also been rewired within him. The story had turned from a dirty secret to a grand prize. You could see this happen in almost every marine that made it past the infancy of their first term: instances of disgrace or extreme debauchery that became enshrined as glorious and heroic in direct proportion to their ugliness, and this shared depravity sharpening the lens through which they judged the world and through which the world in return was precluded from judging them; a refining flame that set them apart from those on the outside, from all those fucking civilians pond-skimming the banal surfaces of their lives. And it bonded them as brothers with the all the permanence and sanctity of a blood pact.

As the last few days drew in Jacko and Smudge were pushing sets of a hundred, a quick shake and a pause at the fifty to keep their arms loose. They were primed and impatient. With three days to run they called time on their routine and they ate double-sized meals with double helpings of dessert to wash it all down and they slept whenever they got the chance and out in the yard they sat about and cleaned their rifles and play-howled along to old dance tunes and there was that easy pleasure of a thing accomplished for which the rewards have not yet been reaped.

The gym was a brick two-room outhouse at the centre of camp. Tongues of cracking paint on the window frames. The memory of a cool, damp smell on the walls; roofing tiles gone flaccid from wintercold and the bulge and strain of long summers. It had that lonely single-mindedness of a place without women.

That day the thermometer on the outer wall cleared an easy forty in the shade. Inside the fans mounted on the corner shelving spoon-churned the air so that the sweat smells from the punch bags and the towelrack slopped in lazy passes back and forth across the room. They hadn't asked for a crowd but several marines had holed up ahead of time, slouching out on upturned plastic packing crates and fist-deep into share bags of tortillas and speaking over each other with goofy, boyish excitement. The war seemed very far away.

The rules were laid down, with Bennett assuming the role of adjudicator and pronouncing the laws of the event with relished and solemn conviction:

Press-ups, gentlemen, to be completed in increments up to a thousand, with rest periods of a maximum of thirty seconds, and the increments not to drop below ten at any time. – Someone complaining, Bennett throwing his hands high as peacemaker – However, *however gentlemen*, the thousand must be completed within an hour to ensure that rest periods are taken only sparingly. Is anyone unclear of the rules?

Old man Buck, one of the gym rats from Lima Company, threw his hat in at the last moment, earning snorts of approval from the gravs shifting twenty kilo stacks on the Smith machine at the opposite end. Various bets were placed: some of the younger marines wagered long lists of sentry duties, Bennett putting himself up against Big Al Henderson to pull an all-nighter in the tower; the sergeant major glancing in under a wide smile (booming: haven't you ladies started yet? I'll serve you scran in my finest lace negligee tomorrow if you can pull it off; fuck it up and you're my admin bitches for the week); Bonzo going toe-to-toe with the boss for that week's allocation of phone minutes, the boss on the point of protesting and Bonzo throwing back a firm, paternal smile: *don't be such a welfare case.*

Who invited these clowns?

Beats me.

You still want to do this?

(Laughing) Do I have a choice?

Not really.

Best get on with it like.

Yeah.

(Pause) Good luck mate.

Nah. Piece of piss. See you at the finish.

They were off before Bennett could finger his stopwatch for the go. They cruised the first hundred in quick bursts of twenty-five, their bodies racing and exalting in the simple familiarity of the movement. Deep-worn passageways of their muscle memories suddenly come alive with colour and mechanical elegance, a fluency of motion that gave an illusion of bone and ligament and tendon and stripe of muscle electing jointly to carry each of them through to effortless completion. Dumb smiles floated on their faces between sets. Less than three minutes in, and with the technical proficiency of the three competitors fully evinced, a dim sense of anti-climax settled amongst those assembled. Muttered distractions and bootshifting began to pepper the quiet that had greeted the start.

Jacko and Smudge set off working in synchronised sets with Buck hulking an offbeat pattern on the third mat. Instinct and long weeks of practise had them unconsciously checking off their progress against the high water mark of their energy reserves. They had learned to structure their sets in a way that exploited the initial trill of strength that would buck them off the tail-end of a rest interval, grabbing maybe a quick easy half dozen before their arms remembered their fatigue. But you couldn't get greedy with it. You had to let your body lead things, to dictate pace and posture. Try and do too much too quickly and it would fail you spitefully like an animal that will not be led.

As they needled towards the three hundred marker Jacko could feel his peak numbers on each set dropping a bald four or five below Smudge's. Their uniform quotient of sets and rests began to drift and patter out of parallel. By three-fifty they were working almost straight alternates, the resting man sitting back into his haunches and flicking his arms out at the wrist and braying useless encouragement and towelling the saltburn out of his eyes. Jacko was coming out of his sets shedding whole skins of sweat that smacked the matting with a pop.

Buck called it quits only twenty shy of the five hundred, bowing low over one hand to the marines still banging their legs against makeshift chairs. He swallowed a bottle of sports drink and walked over to the gravs on the bench slow-clapping him in. He flexed his arms at the elbow and curled his fingers one at a time until the knuckles cracked. Fuck me, fellas. I'm done.

Twenty-four minutes had passed.

The strain was there in the way their faces boiled red on the last two or three and the electric trace of vein on their temples that shuddered there even while they were catching air and shaking out and leaning into their heels. Their shirts hung off them dark and heavy and slopped the mats, forcing them to stuff the wet hems in behind the waistband of their shorts. They were down to about fifteen press-ups a set and gulping down the maximum thirty second rests to search out some fight before the next round swung in. Their sets chicaned in and out of time with each other with jumbled regularity, all focus narrowing to the pinpoint of the next break, the next motion. They forgot each other. They forgot the thinning crowd. They hit six hundred. They hit seven. And each set they lied to themselves that *this one* would be the last, or that *this one* wasn't fifteen any longer: an easy cluster of three fives without a break; five threes perhaps. That seemed reasonable enough. They counted downwards. They counted to ten and silently argued the last three or four or five away as inconsequential, small fry. The lies never held up for long. Jacko's incremental sets fell to the minimum ten.

They were now very far in and the gym was repopulating with marines who had been present for the start and had left to attend working parties or pressing email exchanges, and who were returning out of curiosity or to warm up their own evening sessions. Upturned crating and salted foil wrappers and cola bottles beached the concrete around the front where Jacko and Smudge heaved and snorted through closed teeth and spilled water off their chins into the mats, Bonzo looking up intermittently from a wormy copy of The Republic over the wire of unreal spectacles asking would they mind keeping it down please, some of us are trying to improve ourselves?

Jacko's hands slipped and shucked. Lactic burn budding his arms and shoulders and sockets like a ragged wire dredging deep the irrigation of his veins. Those parts of him not rattling with pain had settled into a buzzed numb. Pins and needles crackled the pads of his fingers. Each and every press-up now requiring singular attention, every one a small mountain of its own. Hitting eight-twenty might have seemed somehow fantastic looking up from where he'd knelt at the startline; now it seemed as far from the finish, as utterly pitifully irrelevant, as any other milestone he had blundered past on the climb.

The clock was draining. Frustration and effort made angry tears stiffen behind his eyes. A high point of four or five at best. The sixth sluggish and uneven, seven and eight making his arms tremble again, and he was holding breaks between the nine and the ten with his buttocks arched into the air and his shoulders heaving and his face boiling. *Ten*. He took his legs out from under him and slumped against the cool matting. Eight-fucking-hundred-and-thirty. Smudge well ahead. Smudge just then tickertaping the big nine-oh-oh. The homeward stretch. Jacko blinked up at Smudge through misted eyelashes and his eyes spoke very clearly. Smudge was throwing his arms out, all of the grace now gone from the movement so they fluttered limp and stringy like flags in the wind.

Smudge spoke quick and quiet. His voice was strange. Calm, somehow. It went under the currents of noise babbling against the blood-heavy wadding of his ear drums.

Come on mate. You've done worse than this.

It was an act of grace. And then he was gone again, lost in the tumult of battles unseen.

He was right. Just another ten. Jacko had learned and relearned it many times before, and each time it became something he knew again for himself in a sharper light of certainty. Ownership of himself had become a testing of the half-life of his own disbelief: always diminishing but always there. Just another ten. That's all it was. That's all it ever was. He hauled himself up onto his arms so that his shoulders sang to the quick and his wrists rattled where they spiked the mat, a dull endorphin afterglow just taking the edge off the bite. Three whole-body breaths and then a start:

One.

Jacko broke a thousand with Smudge counting him in on both hands and one of the lads withdrawing a stealthy toe from his ankles where he'd looked to put him off balance at nine-nine-nine. Bennett prodding the clock from where he was seated and calling time. Fifty-six minutes. Lucky bastard. There were muted congratulations from the stippled spread of onlookers (good effort lad, now stop moaning like a big girl), and Bonzo calling aimlessly out behind a series of moving bodies (will someone find the boss and tell him he owes me thirty minutes' phone time with his wife?) and there was that late bloom of shame that shadows the naked revelations of immense physical exertion. And afterwards, a sense of dull normalcy dewing up out of the dark of their tiredness. Business as usual. It was always the same: finish something and soon enough it was hard to imagine it ever being otherwise.

Smudge blowing, hauling Jacko to his feet by his forearm: well that was a bit fucking cheeky like, hey?

That evening they spoke little over dinner and they slept hungry dreamless sleep and then it was the next morning and the two of them crouched shoulderward over steaming mugs and the sergeant major sashaying high-heeled through the dining hall to plate up breakfast to great whoops and heckles and throated uproar and shortly after midnight Jacko was putting rounds into the engine block and windscreen of an axel-weighted Corolla gone clean through a snap vehicle checkpoint on the road north to Chah-e Anjir.

*

After the war Smudge would find work cleaning and selling fish out of a catering van on the harbour front. He was outside and working civvy street full-time before their second Christmas home. Jacko would go on to be a successful lifer right up until the time of the accident. And it is strange to think that, after everything that happened between them, the day Smudge left the Corps would also be the very last day he would see Jacko, excepting a troop reunion on the fifth year where they would stalk each other hesitantly at the bar before slowly easing themselves into the moulded and still-warm roles of the past. They would drink together that night with Jacko setting the pace and they would share again those charged glances turned against the world and to an outsider it was as if they might never have spent a day apart in their lives. And people would always ask Smudge, do you still stay in touch with your old buddies from the war? You must make the most powerful friendships in such a godawful place. And Smudge would nod and reassure them, playing the part demanded of him, yeah, I still see the guys. I see them all the time. How could I not?

dem dry bones, and death is a very particular smell, an abstract made nearly into wholeness by the very particularity of its abstractions, like a word jagged with consonants or an idea exacted by the loosing of blood; and my fingers are pungent with garlic and butter, I am in a habitual pose of concentration, the tips of them pressed lightly to my lips and jaw, the garlic butter the stubborn remnants of lobster served to us at lunch from the abandoned US PRT freezer stores, fat and white and fleshy and its juices run warmly down our wrists we ate with something a little like astonishment thinking those americans know how to do war thinking bet there are guys here haven't even tasted a fucking prawn before and here they sit scranning down great hunks of white fat desert warzone lobster, absurdity heaped on absurdity something like a double-negative; and we are gathered around a bank of grainy greyscale screens with our faces lit and flickering and the CO at the apex also in a pose of severe concentration and dread has settled like a sick man among us, we watch grainy taliban advance upon the afghan patrol and the soldiers are dragging their dead and wounded and scattering into a disorderly retreat and we watch: we watch the taliban steal away a single soldier, someone behind me breathes jesus, in the tented gloom there is the noise from the radio patching through the attack helicopter and the ops officer calling out coordinates from the maptable and the options are few and too disagreeable to be spoken aloud, and my fragranced fingers are a small obscenity, a rejoinder that we should have dishonoured death by eating our lunch in levity and forgetfulness (it is a common superstition that to hold death always before you is to rob it of that sport in which it most keenly delights); and a week earlier I had visited a hospital on the outskirts of the town with the MO and we had been taken to see the ward and then the mortuary and the smell and the presence of it was there even at the top of the stairs, they peeled the blanket away and it was a policeman that had been taken and cut and shot and eventually burned and dumped roadside by a school, he is black now, rigid as firewood, those are holes that were his eyes, and I had that song swimming my head, dem bones dem bones, and death is very particular and it is a real and present thing: it is pork and it is soot and it is a slight sweetness, something like penny sweets staling in sunlight, and I felt the breath disgorge from my lungs like stringed handkerchiefs in a magic show; and we watch the grey grained screens and the CO nods and he says – take them out – and he nods again, and we watch the taliban and the soldier obliterate in a white whoosh of hellfire and a wholeness does then become an abstraction, violence and fire turned to grainy screens and white noise, the flicker of light on drawn faces, and we will not think of this when we go to sleep tonight, we will turn our hearts away from it as surely as if they had eyes to be closed or ears to be stopped; and we will think of the seaside and we will think of ferris wheels and we will think of lobster

He sets them out in a square in the forecourt and passes around cold bottles of Fanta that bead cold in the hand and quickly go hand-warm. They drink slowly. The drink goes from sweet to syrup in only a few mouthfuls. Mid-afternoon is a cataract of hot white stone and powder and white plastic glare, all of it pinching up and glassy under a fishbowl UV throb. He has Fat Jimmy the submariner and Lieutenant Alison off to his left, and Vince, disinterested and moody and face-cupped, and Farid the interpreter over to his right. Soldiers and marines hurry the boardwalk between operations tents passing them occasional glances. (HQ seems to run on the principle that time is not precious but a thing already lost, that warfare is a preconfigured exercise in salvage and damage limitation). He had told them to take their time, relax, and he had put out a hand before they could protest: the war will still be here when we get back. This is how he does things, his revolution by degree. He kicks his boots up onto an ornamental log bench and takes a big drink. They speak little. When Farid, apropos of nothing, announces his plans to resettle to the UK, his immediate thought, his instinctive thought, is *good for him*; his second, a little delayed, because he is also clear-thinking and deliberate and commonsensical, is *well doesn't this just have trouble written all the way through it.*

February. Slip slop desert-brown morning sleet.

Captain Charlie 'H' Harrison is a man who takes life seriously. This is well known. People sometimes say he reads too much into things. When he is introduced to the team for the first time Farid is sat up on a desktop watching a YouTube video across the cubicle and pointing and laughing so you can see his chewing gum bouncing about on his tongue. Farid is working ripped skinny jeans and a short-collar biker's jacket despite the heat. He has his thin black hair striped back off his forehead. Two parts Bollywood-slick to one part greaseball rockabilly and one part New Wave glam. H doesn't miss a beat and sticks him a hand. A real privilege, he says in a big, serious voice full of intent and expectation. Farid slides back onto the desk and gives a super white smile and pops a Coke. It is a face that looks as though it has heard this voice many times over on six month rotation.

H was grateful for the promotion and he was grateful for the move to 15 Psychological Operations (PSYOPS) Group (POG) and he was grateful for the staff officer deployment with the Information Exploitation (IX) Group to Lashkar Gah. All those grand names and parenthetic acronyms: a boon for dinnertime conversation and a tidy riposte to the endless watercooler STAB bullshit. But most of all H is grateful because he's been gifted a job that doesn't come ready-loaded for a zero sum play: the war machine is singleminded and slow grinding and it doesn't care much for their self-justifications, and jobs like his come rarer than rocking horse shit. There are marine officers he knows that have squared their consciences by learning to love the killing in a big way, only that love has somehow ended up killing whatever vital thing was keeping them distinct, at a fundamental level, from the war itself. They did not come home well. Not usually. He knows others, mostly those stuck out at the FOBs and platoon houses, who have learned to love each other to similar effect.

But H is lucky. He trades in information and communication and influence. He carves his success in the abstract, by his ability to *shape the moral and intellectual battlespace*, not by numbers, not by bodies. They are fighting for scalps while he is fighting for hearts and minds. His is a victimless education of a target audience he has encountered only rarely beyond the old dhobi wallah tending the laundry store on the far side of camp. Radio broadcasts. Bulkload deliveries of school supplies and sporting equipment. Educational pamphlets. Kids t-shirts badged green with Pashtun ISAF scrawl. That sort of thing. Of course, there have been fuck-ups too. There was the airdropped palette of leaflets that failed to disperse and ended up turning that little girl to paste and months of bad propaganda (hearts and minds! hearts and minds! they crowed in the lunch queue). But these failures are few and H assuages himself with the knowledge that collateral damage is necessary and inevitable (he is eighty to ninety per cent sure this is a Clausewitzian truism), and he tends this particular small and regretful piece of his heart as a war wound as real as any sustained on the battlefield.

March. Sleet into rain into dawnmist and steady forenoon sun. Poppy stiffening in its soil.

H settles into the role quickly. He marks his command of the team with a leadership style he thinks of as a quirky, slightly left-field combination of hard professionalism and laissez faire let-the-work-speak-for-itself man-management. Out of earshot of more senior officers he encourages them to use their Christian names at the expense of rank and formality, a move that thrills softly with the heretical. He orders them out of the office daily for an hour's training regardless of the workload. This always with a Christmas smile. Alison, née Lieutenant Barker-Hyde, is already four months in and responds to this upheaval with a kind of resigned ambivalence, a visible deflation (one common enough amongst the clerical staff to earn its own nickname: the deskbound warrior thousand-yare stare). She is smoking more and there are rumours she is fucking the married HQ adjutant. Vince, the only marine deployed to the POG, seethes slow and bitter and bored at his desk in an unconsummated battlelust as he grapples with tribal atmospherics and key influencers and other nouns *bent the fuck out of shape man*. Through all of this Farid moves untouched and untouchable, like a guard-friendly lifer come floating to the surface through sheer dint of his seniority and squeal value.

Their immediate occupation is a short-term influence op aimed at promoting women's rights across the township and outlying villages. Alison deploys with the soldiers on routine patrols and talks about contraception and education and regional politics and human rights with young wives shuffled out by the menfolk and returned promptly to their curtained, shadowed empires. H judges this strategy a minor success and backfills reams of photography and reporting to the UK for promotional purposes (Vince: propaganda for the propaganda, right? Jimmy: give it a rest mate).

The cubicle is humming with the chug of air-con. A sheer afternoon slats the closed blinds in a stack of laser white lines. Farid is flipping through a folder of proofs and tapping his heel out to an unheard tune. He has his upper lip curled in a curt sneer.

I don't understand.

What's that Fad? Jimmy glancing up over his monitor, mid-mouthful.

I don't understand what it is you are trying to achieve with this project. The schools and the training, yes. I can understand that. But what do you hope to come from this?

Dunno. Equal rights and that? Jimmy shrugs and drops back behind the screen.

But these women, these women don't know anything about the

world or about politics or about science. What can you expect from them? What can you hope for this to achieve?

He pokes the pages stiff-fingered.

That's the point though, isn't it? says Alison, spinning quarterwise in her chair. How can we expect them to achieve anything if we don't educate them? If we don't give them a chance to see a slice of the real world outside of the same old four walls?

Farid laughs like a child. It is a strange and happy and inappropriate Hollywood-borrowed laugh.

You know I am impressed by the work we do. Nearly always. And it is good work. But in this I think you are wrong. – Pause – Really I do. Women should stay at home and they should cook for their men and they should raise their children. It is the way of things, the right way of things. It is the way of things here.

And I suppose you think men have a right to beat women too?

Yes, I think men have a right to beat their women. He says it child-faced, without provocation.

You're a little shit, Fad. You don't know what you're talking about. Alison spins back to the desk and bats at her keyboard blat blat blat and drains her coffee in one cold swill and pockets her lighter and steps outside. A bolt of sunlight that races half a turn clockwise across the walls and sucks back into the yard with the ka-*chunk* of the doorlatch.

H stares down the length of the cubicle and sucks his pen. Farid is leant up still, thumbing the proof copies, the collar of his jacket high on his neck and the hems of his jeans folded twice so they sit flat and cuffed and neat against the laces on his white sports shoes. Cognitive dissonance is what it is. It's the eyes taking in the full Western get-up and the ears getting all that tribal talk that might as well be ten or twenty or a hundred or a thousand years old for all it has to say. That's what makes it sit wrong. But he's thinking, *you've got to respect his honesty,* and, *we can't expect them to drop centuries of cultural baggage just like that,* and, *progression's only ever a steady drip-fed erosion of untruth and misunderstanding, that's all it is.* Farid catches him and drops him this big full-face grin that could just as rightly be a tiger sizing up a small mammal come stumbling out at its feet.

On the wall a calendar page flaps restlessly.

April. The days come in like glue and by night the slither of far-off gunfire sticks and dangles on slow air.

H dines with a regular cohort of marine officers and embassy and GCHQ staff and they take the late shift when the galley is almost emptied of other ranks except for a few solitary soldiers cycling out of sentry duty. Loud table laughs. Cutlery ringing against the opentop. The marines talk with a vicious kind of charm about their day-craft, baiting smiles, stories about using thirty thousand pound Hellfire missiles to strafe fighters caught out in the open, a kind of PlayStation-age bullet dance for militaries with deep pockets and user-friendly rules of engagement; and about the intercept transcripts of the Arab pop star joining the jihad in Helmand only to find that jihad was cold and dirty and wet and involved getting shot at (and eventually shot); and about the regular comedy IED misfires that deglove the Taliban operators whole where they kneel and leave them strewn at the point of detonation like chewed sausage skin with all the meat sucked out. And the embassy staff respond with theatrical astonishment and horror and they rebut with talk of elections and building new roads and firing up the dam at Kajaki, and the whole thing amounts to a daily dance (or a retreat, he can't tell which) on both sides into the predefined, pre-agreed, roles from which they flirt and pout with impunity.

Well, to a point. This is the phrase H likes to use. He says it with his eyes blinking and half-drawn, the start of an affected stutter just threatening on the edge of his tongue. He considers himself a man of the third way. When the OC asks him, Harrison, you're a smart chap, are you going to tell me you side with these tree-huggers and their wild fantasies? Do you honestly think elections can bring any real kind of stability to the tribes? he puts one finger to his lips and lets his eyelids flicker and he replies, *well, to a point*, and in his response he balances liberal ideals with a hard dose of real-world practicality and good ol fashioned common sense and some talk about war being the continuation of policy (also Clausewitzian), and he moves freely and fluidly between the fixed polarisations of his colleagues, his *to a point* like a skeleton key nudging open door after door out into strange and half-familiar ideascapes newly seen and newly understood. In doing so he also secretly considers himself to be a man of history and a prophet.

H is well pleased with these conversations and he is often pleased when he goes to sleep at night. The dinner talks leave him with that happy feeling from when he had been to confession as a boy.

When they stop the extra ration supplies for the Afghan guard force, H calls in a favour from the chief cook and conspires for them a weekly crate of fresh fruit and vegetables and sachets of powdered sauce. It is a practical move, he explains to himself. Can't have the guards on security detail getting mutinous now, can we? He does not tell of it to anyone and that makes it all the sweeter. In the evenings he sometimes sits with the guards for an hour or two and fumbles his basic Pashtun while they laugh and smoke and chow down on the packets of sweets he has brought them from the NAAFI. They name him Yellow Flower and he is also very pleased with this. He comes away with a sense of having made something of the war without surrendering himself entirely to it. This is important in a way he can't yet place.

H also shows himself to be steely when necessary. In the third week of April all local nationals on camp are barred from the gym. There is muttering and closed-mouth belches of dissent and a conciliatory sandbox and volleyball net are thrown up hurriedly outside the Afghan quarter. Farid storms the office for two or three days. H explains to him: I know *you* are fine using the kit, but the simple fact is that the gym equipment is extremely dangerous if it's not used properly. The commandant has a duty of care to everyone on this base, and the truth is that we don't have the time to train the guards *and* keep an eye on them too. It's nothing personal. There's a war on, you know (laughing, a firm double pat on the shoulder). The sweet rank of body odour lifts suddenly from the rowing machines and the bike rack and H allows himself a brief flush of relief, thank god, that he turns to raised eyebrows and pursed lips and an *I-think-that's-quite-enough-don't-you?* loaded smile when he overhears Vince expressing a similar sentiment on his smoke break.

May. Bomb sounds in the market; little florets of rocket fire on the far banks of the river turning to city smoke and sunhaze.

Alison finishes her tour early in the month. H had anticipated a note of solemnity to the occasion, a sense of one chapter closing and another just beginning and of the gentle dredging of bittersweet storybook viscera. But Vince and Jimmy snap playfully at each other as before and Alison's desk and corner is swept clean of person and history in one short afternoon. It is a reminder that he is still new, still not yet fully broken in to the peculiarity and slight misshapenness of wartime living. He escorts her to the helipad on the last day and dumps her bags hangar-side, the downwash from the Chinook shaking them in alternate slabs of cool and oven-warm air, and she slips him a formal handshake and says, yes, well good luck, stay in touch, eh? and strides over to the crewman at the tailgate through exhaust stripes and violent heat shimmer and she doesn't look back. *Well good luck*. He feels a little cheated.

The days start to creak.

They have a new Lieutenant Carter join the team. He hasn't yet earned his Christian name. He is full of ideas and H says to the others, it's great to have a bit of vibrancy and enthusiasm round here, don't you think? But god – smiling behind one hand – that Lieutenant Carter is a bit fucking wet behind the ears. This makes them laugh.

H is putting in an early hour before the team file through from the breakfast run. Outside the day is pink-splashed and ripening and in the cubicle there are still traces of the cool unmovement of the night lightly touching at the edges of things. He drinks his coffee. He reads.

Farid bursts through and leaves the door banging twice behind him on its frame. He fires up his computer where he stands. He is swaying and skittish and his fingernails rattle the deskwork while the computer clicks into life. H watches him over the nose of his paperwork, takes a loud sip of coffee. Farid pushes some papers around on his desk. After only a few seconds he seems to take hold of himself and he crosses back along the length of the cubicle and he presents himself square and centred in front of where H is sat.

I need to talk to you.

I thought you might.

It is very serious.

Take a seat.

Farid kicks himself out into an office chair and shuffles his feet for a time and stares at the toes of his shoes. He does not look H direct in the face.

It happened last night. On my way home from work. I usually take the long route. It is about forty or fifty minutes to walk, even though my family lives less than half a mile away. It is safer this way. So no one will know I have come from here.

Ok.

I had been walking for about twenty minutes, I think. I reached the junction at the north end and I followed it round so I was coming back into the city from the west. I had the sun behind me. As I was turning off the main road I noticed I was being followed by two men on motorbikes. They stayed about two hundred metres behind me the whole time. I lost them once or twice in traffic. But I found them again. Or they found me.

H leans forward over steepled fingertips, his face flattening.

It was getting dark, especially going back into the city. As I turned off the main road they came at me quickly. Out of nowhere. They grabbed me and dragged me into an empty road. One of them had me like this – he screws a fist around the collar of his shirt – and the other was hitting me in the side of the head.

My god. Are you alright?

I am fine. They didn't take off their helmets so I couldn't see their faces. But they handed me this note. – Farid uncrumples a sheet of yellow paper from his pocket and smooths it out against the desk with the heel of his palm – It says: you are working with the foreigners, who are the enemies of religion and Islam. You take money from them. You should be fearful of God. Every day, you shake hands with the infidels and you make yourself impure in their presence. This is a warning. You will stop this otherwise we will take such action against you that a Muslim has not yet done to another Muslim. And then they left.

They left? Just like that?

He nods.

H blows through closed lips and leans back into his chair and works his jaw muscles.

Farid, this is extremely serious. I will need to raise it with the commandant immediately. – He pauses; runs a finger under his nose – But thank you for telling me. You did the right thing.

He nods again.

And you're sure you're ok?

Fine, I suppose. But I am worried. For my family.

Of course you are. Let me make some calls, find out what the next steps need to be.

I cannot stay here and work here and put them at risk like this.

I know. Best thing for you to do now is to go grab yourself a drink and cool down and let me talk to the right people. We can fix this.

It is not worth the risk, not to them, not for the money –

Farid flicks up his face as he says this and it is the first time that morning that their eyes catch and H goes suddenly still in his chair and in the next moment he is moving again and scratching at his morning beard and making nonsense shapes with his lips. A long silence hangs between them.

Where did you say they hit you in the face again? H studies him close, bobbing his head to catch the light on Farid's skin.

My face? No, they hit me in the head, at the back *here*. With closed fists, like this. Only a few times. To scare me, maybe.

Pause.

Ok. Leave it with me.

That evening, over dinner, H describes how his bloody interpreter had tried to wrangle a bloody pay rise out of him and he describes how the boy almost had him, I mean, really almost suckered me in, and it wasn't a bad fist at the story by any stretch, the kid's got brains alright, he just got greedy and chased onto the money thing too early and suddenly the whole scam is clear as daylight. They laugh and roll their eyes and he feels pleased again and a little ashamed.

One afternoon in the last week of that month they are sitting out in the forecourt when Farid announces his plans to resettle to the UK. Afterwards H is reminded of what Clausewitz said about war being a dangerous business and about the mistakes coming from kindness being the very worst for it.

June. Dogs shallow-breathing in the belly of a midday ditch. Rumours of spies within the city walls.

Vince is caught in a roadside blast on only his second patrol and he is rushed back to the UK and the doctors are unable to save his right arm and he is in a coma for three weeks before they are able to begin assessing the extent of brain trauma. The whole situation should reel with irony, except the war has a way of putting a splash of random right through the substance of things so that it rinses out any sign of the agency of certainty and purpose on which irony depends. There's just too much chance, too many billions of other ways it could equally have gone to ratshit.

The effect on the team is profound. It leaves them dazed and scattered and unsure of themselves so that they too feel they have somehow lost a limb, that they too must learn to live and work afresh out of the scorched earth of their trauma. And it signals an end to the entente cordiale H enjoyed as mediator slipping between the clotted, shifting membranes of war and peace; an act of aggression forcing him take up arms for a cause that has already claimed him for itself. When he sits to dinner he no longer courts his revolutionary-reactionary middle way but is distant and distracted. Inarticulate. He feels somehow battle-hardened by proxy. They never say it but he feels the marines have now seized on him as one of their own. And he finds some comfort in this, deep in his corkscrew out of the open skies of neutrality.

The Battle Group is making decent headway in the northern and southern main AOs when intelligence begins to nod towards the soft rot right there at the heart of the province. Reports show a day-on-day increase in fighters transiting through Babaji and Wazir Kalay and Mirmandab and up along the slate-green flatlands north of the river into Nahr-e Saraj. And across camp there is apparent suddenly a deep earnestness that is uncommon and touching and faintly ridiculous; a surface disturbance betraying the movement of vast, slow shapes far below.

The entire strategy is adjusted in preparation for a third front. The team start working thirteen, fourteen, fifteen hour shifts. H cancels their obligatory training sessions. The tone of the work also changes. Instead of the soft engagement projects and photo calls they begin drafting evacuation leaflets to be confetti spread over the villages in advance of a pre-emptive operational thrust. They prepare written statements for the company interpreters to megaphone across no-man's land to put the fear of Allah into spider-trenched foot soldiers and working-aged males and farmhands armed with fifty-year-old Kalashnikovs. In secret they are prospected to design cardboard tokens for a US Special Forces unit to place on dead men's eyes, coins richly bevelled with hand-drawn skulls and scythes and badass grim reapers wearing belts of ammo over stars and stripes cassocks and smoking hip-mounted

M249 SAWs. (Not a plan that gets very far past the fucken limey prudes at Brigade Headquarters). They work late into the nights and by about eleven or twelve Jimmy has taken to flicking over from Sky News to MTV. Farid snarls at the women in their half-undress and he cannot tear his eyes away.

Where before the war had impinged on H as a nuisance, something to endure, now it is sleeping and eating and living that he finds impinging upon his war. A transformation common enough during these hungry months. At times he feels the intensity and the vitality and the movement of it all has kept him healthy, kept him whole, as though he has been borne gingerly over spoiling seas and bad winds. He finds it is something like being in love and the songs on the TV late into the night all seem to have special weight to them, a special and uncertain significance. They stir a deep part of him. When the offensive begins he wrings his hands in the command centre like a penitent and a part of him makes a small prayer that none of it will ever end.

Farid applies for resettlement through the formal channels and receives his rejection notice on the thirtieth. In it the commandant writes that a committee had reviewed his claim and that, whilst *some merit* had been found to support resettlement, current regulations did not generally allow for wholesale resettlement to the UK except in highly unusual circumstances. He is encouraged to resubmit his application in nine months' time.

July. Soft spoors of light throbbing against hillshadow on the night horizon; the war always beautiful viewed at a distance and through plastic screen windows.

I'm sorry. There's nothing I can do.

But there must be something.

I'm sorry. H turns out his hands in apology and shuffles his hips in the swivel chair and puts out a long loud breath. The corner-mounted TV jangles with pop tunes he knows down to the fibre, though he can hardly tell name or lyrics or singer.

I have been here for more than two years now. I have dedicated myself to my work. And now I am in danger none of you will help me. *Now* you decide to throw me to the wolves.

Farid. – Another sigh – You know very well it's not like that. They will have taken great deliberation over your case. And the signs are promising. Really they are. This is just a short-term setback, that's all.

But that is no good to me *now* and it is *now* that I need your help.

Look. You knew the dangers for yourself when you signed up. You think your situation is unique? That you're the only person to face hardship or suffering in all this? None of this should come as a surprise to you, to any of us. We've all had to sacrifice. – Softening some; catching breath; one hand placed over his – Listen to me, Farid. We can help you. Let me try and push through your papers and have you reassigned to another PRT. Maybe we can get you posted out to Kandahar or Oruzgan. Get you away from all this.

And what about my family and friends?

Like I say, it's a short-term solution. Nothing perfect. But it's a start.

You expect me to start again? To start over so that I am unknown, so that in another two years I will be in exactly this position again? Saying these same things and begging someone else to listen to me?

I am listening to you.

Farid crosses his arms. Blazes.

And let's not forget, you are being well paid for your troubles, for the risk. I'm sure there are people outside this base right now that would consider killing their own mothers for the sort of money you take home.

Well paid? Well paid? I get two hundred pounds a month. You think that is well paid when I want to start my life again in England? What will that buy me? Tell me? Or are you also on two hundred pounds a month? – And then, delivered with care and poise and a neatly judged jab of spite – *Sir*.

H flinches like he's taken a glancing sock to the chin. A deep inhalation.

Farid. I sympathise with you. I sympathise with you enormously. You are a hugely talented individual and an asset to this team. I for one am tremendously proud to have worked alongside you. Tremendously *honoured*. Shit, – laughing now so his shoulders heave right to his earlobes – if I had my way, my friend, I'd have you working out of this office until the war was over.

He considers this a nice diplomatic touch; a regain after the clumsy misstep down the whole pay and money culvert. No need to become overly preoccupied with the insolence. He doesn't mean it. He's just emotional. And rightly so. I can get that.

Bullshit, says Farid, spit frothing his bottom lip. You British have a duty of care towards me and my family for what I have done for your country.

Bullshit and *duty of care*. H cannot think how either phrase made it into Farid's idiosyncratic vocabulary. They stick and grind like hot coals high in his throat making his collar warm, his cheeks flush.

Now don't you take that tone of voice with me young man –

No. This is bullshit. I'm sick of you liars, you war lovers. You're all the same. You promise everything but you only really care about yourselves and about your careers and about getting away from here as fast as you can. – His head shakes from side to side as though giving space for his words and tongue to catch the race of this thoughts, his eyes bulging – And *you*. You're the worst of them all. At least the others accept that they are playing their games, at least they know it is all lies and pretending. But you, you look at me like I'm something that came out of the sewers, something you brought in on your boots. You walk around here like you know better than anyone else, like you're above all this. But I'll tell you something, sir. You're not. – Pause – You're as guilty as any of us. Maybe more so. At least we live with the bad things. Sometimes, sometimes I even think you might be glad about what happened to Mr Vince –

H has him pinned against the wall in one clean movement, Farid's neck tight and swallowing in the web of his thumb and index finger. He is surprised at how light the boy feels in his hand, as though his little jiggling marionette bones are gas-blown full of helium. The smack of aftershave on his clothes.

Now you listen carefully you primped up little fuck. You think you know it all but you don't. You think a couple of years working out of here makes you a big man? Someone important? Pah. You may as well have come up out of the sewers for all I care. For all anyone cares. And if you ever even *think* to speak that way to me again I'll have you fired and back on the streets and sucking cock to pay your bills so fucking quickly you won't even have time to wipe the snot off your nose. Do you hear me?

Pause.

And then…a flicker across his face, a shiver of movement so slight it hides itself in stillness. And Farid bursts out laughing.

It is late. H sits with one closed fist to his lips, his free hand tip-tapping at a mug of tea long since cooled to grey milky platelets. A warm night presses the sheeted windowglass and there is the sound of the generators thudding like beaten sackcloth outside. The silence in the cabin seems to thrum, seems to shake slightly on its own. He sits there and he argues a fine defence for himself against a lazy and irrational and drunk-bellowy prosecution but it only makes him sicker. The things the boy said come back at him, sharpening with each carefully deployed slice of logic and rebuke, each, yes, to a point, until they have hardened irrevocably and become not an accusation but a truth, and then not a truth but a Truth, until they press softly and consistently on his conscious like sunshapes blotted onto black eyelids. Where his reason fails him something else slithers and crowns in its place. He thinks of the boy and his ignorant farmhand mannerisms, that way he has of parading his absurd costumes with a bellyful of entitlement, of barely masked disdain, and of his Hollywood-dumb blinkers on the world that he actually considers a form of worldliness, and of his dirty mean-spirited religion and its dirty mean-spirited evangelists, and of every one of those stupid cheating lying creatures across this sick and wasting land... And he soaks himself in this until he can hear himself grinding his back teeth in the quiet of the room. His heart light and untroubled in a way he had forgotten or perhaps never quite known.

August. Brize winds. Airfield grass showing blue through a low-country fog.

we took out east on highway one until the day scurried the shadows beneath the rocks and we put in a fishhook and set the guns on the high ground overlooking the pass and the men sat and rested in the cool of a withered cypress grove, smoking and drinking warm bottles of water and singing like boys, and I went with bonzo and we consulted our maps against that barren inscrutable aspect of the valley beneath us: the ruins of a town like strewn wood coals and the sheer valley walls and the wrinkled scarline of some ancient rivercourse: maiwand, I told him: and I saw too, the river running full again, the sun heavy upon a land that glints and tremors and smokes and delights once more in the great festivity of battle; and I see them, men out of seam with the wholeness of their oblivion, they thumb the cartridges clumsily into their carbines and they fire without aim and they run as if falling; they are shot where they stand, and the medic covers the eyes of the wounded with his forearm and he puts their brains out where they lie and then that even is a mercy too far and the wounded are swallowed alike by gunsmoke, by the unearthly sounds of horses screaming that covers them; and there the lieutenant falls them back along a shallow nullah to a garden in a village called khig, and then through the bodies he falls them back again to a second garden where the bullets on the mud walls blot them from the sun, and even as they behold the blade of the enemy he feels all the living within him braced up indignant and disbelieving, that surely he shall be exculpated yet by god or fate, that this cup might pass him by, and he recognises this in himself and he is ashamed and it is this he carries into eternity, into false immortality where the memories of him and his eleven, like their bones, are picked by the sandwinds that turn unceasingly the surface of the earth; and what to stand in their place but an effigy, cast-iron collossus, a lion stood powerfully into its brazen pose, patriated in an english garden too mannered either to temper its hubris or do it proper glory, where roses quaint the flower beds like elderly women, planted in strong crimson rows as if to honour mighty malalai who did sing that day of the roses shamed by the beauty of the blood that did fall, and the roar of the lion bellows now above their lost calls, but if you could hear them, those whispers that are like the scrambled boxsignals that tell obliquely of the beginnings and the edges of the universe, you would not hear them gladdened of their rest but calling for one moment more amongst the living, for how can the dead be at peace when death is so utter? and we went down and the men were singing still in the thin shelter of the trees and we kitted up and moved out and there was a lightness upon them that afternoon that came without cause or precedent and it was like the fighting had fled them and they were little children, knowing only the sun's slow arc and a small and pleasant hunger in their bellies and the wind on the highway and today

During the worst of the fighting we had guys unloading palettes of plywood coffins against the suck and downdraft of the helicopters peeling out of the landing site. We were storing them in our watercooler units until they could be shipped off. They were a uniform six-feet in length and you had to think about how they managed to jam the bigger guys in there. Other times you had to wonder what they managed to fill a six-foot plywood box with at all. One of the guys told me once you could tell the way things had gone down just by how the boxes sat on your shoulders. You don't want to be thinking too much about that kind of stuff.

And you could tell these coffins had been assembled in a hurry: all jagged ends and overhanging lips and the nails in the lids banged through aslant so they split the finish on the side panels. They were almost cartoon comic. That made them all the more terrible somehow. If you were a pen-pusher like me and you'd missed the excitement during the day you would always know the fighting had gone bad when the door to the watercooler was locked up. That was just the way things were that summer.

It had been one of those days. I found Brammers back in the accommodation pod sitting at the end of his cot. He had an old towel laid out on the floor in front of him. There was a bag of peanuts next to his boots and an open pack of Marlboro reds.

I stood in the doorway and watched him pop the pins on his rifle and ease out the spring and working parts so they spilled into a pile on the towel. His hands were black with grease. He didn't look up at me.

You know half the stuff they taught us was wrong?

He wasn't asking, not really. I knew that straight off.

He polished up the bolt carrier and held it lengthways to the light to spot for grit filing in the bore. He shuffled his boots on the matting and I caught the blue plastic of a half-empty bottle sided just past the block of his heel.

Remember in recruit training? Remember how we were told to keep our rifles bone-dry fighting in the desert? Only the slightest drop of oil to ease it all along, right? It's bullshit. You keep these things dry and I promise you, I fuckin promise you, you'll catch a stoppage right on the money, right when you need it most.

He held the carrier between his fingers and he looked it over slow and particular and his index finger went smoothing across one face and he sniffed deep, satisfied, and laid it square on the towel and he picked up the bolt. He looked at me. His eyes pinked at the edges.

You'd think they were trying to kill us, all the bullshit we've been fed. Nope. It's simple. You've got to drown these things in oil. Forget about smoking your position out. You've got to have it dripping so it flushes all the dirt and shit through. She won't let you down when she's wet. It's just like your chick back home. Get her wet and she'll just keep on firing all night long.

Pause.

Mate, this place stinks. I can smell it on you.

He stopped wiping down the bolt and he looked at his boots and across at the bottle laying on its side and then he carried on wiping. I don't want to hear it.

If they catch you like this we're both in the shit.

I said I don't want to hear it.

How much?

Huh?

How much did you get through?

Of that? There's enough left for you. Cool yourself. Have some.

You shouldn't be going through my stuff.

Cool yourself. It's no biggie. There's enough left to get your mouth wet on.

82

Camp was technically dry but every fucker had a scam going. Our girlfriends had taken to sending out drink in mouthwash bottles to get them through RAF customs. I was getting vodka or whisky sent out every few weeks. Brammers' missus had been sending out eighteen per cent sweet liquor but it had given us none of the hit and all of the thick head the next day and he had asked her to drop it and he was keeping me sweet with belt-fed porn in exchange for open access to my stash. I was getting killed on the exchange rate.

Where are the others anyway?

He didn't say anything. He pulled out a small spray bottle from his cleaning kit and worked the oil deep inside the trigger housing and along the rails and over the bolt and spring and carrier and gas parts until the pieces shone thinly in the batterylight. Laid out in aggregate that way, at clean right angles to each other and parallel to the threading on the towel, it gave the impression of having been commissioned for that purpose alone. The rifle whole just a lucky fluke. Brammers stared at it, distracted. He cracked the knuckles on his right hand one after the other against the heeled palm of his left and he worked himself back the other way. Then he started snapping it back together.

So are you going to tell me what happened or what?

A long fuckin day is what happened. What do you think?

Pause.

Whatever.

I stepped out from the air-con of the pod into a wall of ovenwarm air and darkness and nighttime city smells and there was that sudden dumb feeling of being on holiday abroad that died off as quickly as you knew it was there. Outside the accommodation there was a thin strip of dirt and a wall of Hesco damping the sides of the tent from mortar splash. Two plastic office chairs with a pile of magazines stacked underneath. A coffee table fashioned out of two wooden fruit crates with Peshawar stencilled across the sides that Brammers had lifted from behind the kitchen and patiently crafted into shape. A hot wind was blowing through and it was dirty and full of shrapnel and purifying and it was hard to shake the feeling that somewhere out in the darkness it was combing the branches of unseen and sandblasted trees.

I crossed my boots on the table and paged through one of the magazines by the half-light. I didn't have much interest. There was muffled laughter somewhere down the line and a movement of torchflash making the shadows from the pylons and the Hesco cages stand out sharp in the dust and the darkness. Brammers was out soon enough. He paced the rigging lines that marked the edges of our makeshift garden with his hands in his pockets and his face arched up into the night. He tiptoed a quick view over the Hesco and he trailed a slow and lazy circuit back round to me and he sat himself openlegged and casual and he sniffed and passed a glance at me kind of curious and kind of surprised. As though coming upon me there marked some unusual turn of chance. He handed me the bottle and I took a drink and I handed him the bottle and he took a drink and things were ok between us.

I closed my magazine and tossed it folded onto the table.

I saw the vehicle you brought back in with you.

The police wagon?

Yeah.

Not much to look at, is it?

Looked pretty fucked, what with the sides all punched in. I'm surprised you didn't just junk it.

There wasn't space to carry them with us so the boss had the bright idea of towing them behind in that blown-out lump of shit. Can you believe that? And get this: we're crawling along at twenty with the towcable stretched out to absolute fuckin breaking point (two of them have already gone and we're ripe to get hit again at any moment), and honest to god, these clowns in the police wagon are having a right old ramadan of a time giggling and screaming and bouncing about and tickling each other like a bunch of schoolgirls on a day trip to the seaside.

I laughed. He gunned me a look.

He poured himself a capful and put it back in one.

So what happened?

So we were down in the village by dawn, right. We spoke with some farmers by the river. We spoke to the village elder. The usual shit. They wanted us to put a bridge in to open their main routes into town and we haggled and promised a load of stuff we probably don't intend to deliver any time soon. Then we headed out west to a point where the tracks got all narrow and the vehicles kept getting wedged in between the canal and the compound walls.

He lit a cigarette and offered me the pack and I said I was trying to quit and he said he was too and laughed, and he sucked on his cigarette and blew it off to one side. The generator lamps putting spokes through it.

It was a stupid place to be. Fuckin toppers with poppy. We shouldn't have been poking around. Any idiot could have seen it.

He took a drink straight from the bottle and coughed blinking into a closed fist saying *whoo-ey*. He wiped his lips on the back of his forearm, blinked his eyes dry.

Here, pass me some more of that, I said.

So the track opens out into this valley, right, with a row of compounds up along the other side. We're dropping into it when I hear this crack and from across the way a fuckin RPG goes out over our heads and I'm standing there watching its little smoketail like an idiot and suddenly there's gunfire opening up on the front vehicles. Everything just turns into this big noisy mess. We had vehicles reversing into ditches and wheel-spinning the mud and guys in black pyjamas and red bandanas (*red fuckin bandanas*, exclamation-marking each word with a jab of his cigarette) jumping out from cover and hosing us with AK fire. That's some mad shit right there.

Brammers smoked. The drink had got him talky. He was looking loose and relaxed and he was throwing off loose gestures with his words and he was telling it with a mean smile. That also seemed to help the telling.

And we're doing this kind of slow backwards crawl out of the valley and trying to get the fire down only you can hear the bullets pinging off the bonnet. Like, I never thought they would actually do that, you know? Fuck knows how no one caught it up down there. We shouldn't have been there in the first place and we sure as shit didn't know what to do when it all turned nasty. But we got away with it. – Laughing, shaking his head sorrowfully from the neck – One way or another we got away with it.

He finished his cigarette and lit another direct from the stub and settled himself back into his chair.

So after that we played Wacky Racers across town and into the next and out into the desert. They had our number. Ha. They had our fuckin number alright. The convoy was belting it out of there and they were still managing to hit us every two or three hundred metres. Guys just standing up out of the poppy, mega chilled-like, spraying at us at point blank range. I was watching rockets going straight between the vehicles. You could smell rocket smoke on the fuckin cabin air-con, mate. It was a shooting gallery down there.

He stopped, settled himself.

That was when the police wagon took the hit. Spun off into a ditch and threw them clear of the wreck.

Brammers looked off. He took another drink and grit his teeth against the bite. He stood and stretched off his arms one after the other over his chest and he paced the dirt in loping shuttles that put up the dust about his boots. The night was pitchy and thick and the tented light was soft on it and his profiled face looked strangely pale even in that softness.

What were we even doing there? That's what I can't figure. I mean, is this it? Is this our big plan for winning the war? It's like we haven't got the first fuckin idea of what to do or how to do it and we're still cuffing every little detail on the fly. And what really sticks in my throat are these officers sitting miles behind the frontline with their fuckin maps and their fuckin coffee and their fuckin felt-tips and none of them with even a minute of triggertime to their names. What gives them the right to play dice with us? What gives them the fuckin right?

He snorted and spat into the dirt.

So what happened?

What do you mean what happened?

I mean how did you get out of it? What did you do?

What we always do. We drove, mate. We fuckin drove. All those years of training, all that elite commando bullshit, and the best we can do when we get in the shit is stick the pedal to the floor and hotfoot it back to camp, tail between our legs. It's a joke.

And that's it?

Pause.

Yeah. That's it.

I don't get it.

There's nothing to get.

So what are you getting yourself all worked up over? Shit happens. Everyone made it home today. That's got to count for something.

You don't get it, do you? You don't get it at all. Sitting on your arse all day with Brigade. You think the war's just about a fuckin *body count*?

Brammers was getting still and tight in on himself. He lit another cigarette and leant up against the Hesco, turning himself away from me. I could see his jaw muscles working. He turned on his heel and paced the length of the rigging lines twice and then he stopped, head down, and rocked in his boots. His leg jabbed out faster than my eye could catch and his boot went clean through the roughwood apron of the coffee table. The table crumpled, a tin of poker chips scoring a slow sad incline towards the break in the centre before upending itself over the ground.

Ah fuck it.

He poked at the table with his toe cap and stepped back a couple of paces and studied it from a near distance. Sort of thinking it through. Whatever had got him riled up like that was already out of him, already forgotten. He had something of the look of a person witnessing an accident. Now look what I've done.

Leave it. It's just a shitty old crate.

That took me two afternoons to fix up.

Brammers bent to the table and he tested the pieces where they hinged on their nails. He lined up the clean serrations of the break and brought them apart again. He flexed the surface out of its deformity, pushing his fist from underneath and easing the surface crack into flatness. His fingers were easy and considered against the tablegrain. A kind of particularity of touch, a consideredness, that I remembered thinking was just him overcompensating for the drink and not getting it at all.

Leave it mate.

He ground his cigarette out and went back inside and I picked up the magazine and thumbed through to where I had left off and when he came back out I watched him over the pages. He was carrying nails between his teeth and a claw hammer. I asked him where he'd got a hammer from and he looked at me like I was simple and he told me through closed teeth that he'd got it from the toolbox, what did I fuckin think? and I decided it wasn't worth starting something over so I just nodded and let it drop.

He went down on one knee in the dirt and set his tools beside him. He clawed out the old nails where the break had bent them in their sockets and he put two new nails clean through the butt joint on each leg and he gathered the snub discarded nails in a neat pile. It pulled the apron out straight and brought the break into rough alignment. He went back inside and returned with a roll of black tape. Two sheets of thick cardboard. He bent the cardboard back on itself and ran his fingernails along the crease and he turned the table on its overside and pressed the surface through until it ran flush along the seam of the wood.

I watched Brammers in his fixing. A quartermoon broke the dark over us licking our nearness into light and shadows, Brammers bowed there at the spotlighted centre straining himself to his task. He had big eyes on it and his hands worked the wood in firm and fatherly gestures and there was a kind of madness to it all, as though perhaps he hoped by his efforts to mend some deep brokenness in the workings of the world. In his own hidden workings. There was a lot of madness back then, enough that it was easy not to notice, and sometimes easier still to forget. It was often a hard thing to tell apart from virtue, from courage, and virtue too had a habit of getting lost or unnoticed and ending up forgotten forever. The same way I would forget that which I taken for his madness as soon as the clouds returned to hurry the moonlight away.

It was quiet out.

Where are the others anyway? I asked again.

He didn't look up.

In the morning Brammers' cot was empty and his boots were gone. Normal patrol patterns were up and running. At breakfast I drank two cups of coffee and ran through the night's reports and I thought some more about the war. By noon the watercooler was unlocked.

and this: it is a word they disavow reflexively, a little defensively, like children instincting trickery in the sudden open meadow of some simple-seeming adult entreaty, and the others will see only modesty in this disavowal and that modesty will be a proof to them of the very rightness of their judgement (and it is not a distinction easily spurned but it sticks and sullies like an aspersion); and back then I once said almost the exact same, sitting there with an amused smile and an amused paternal pose while he's there with his elbows on the desk and a face like he's been asked to pull the fucking cord on his dear old grandmother, he cracks his knuckles weakly (there's no better phrase for it, he is actually wringing his hands, he strains the soft small fingerbones like a rag) and he does not look me quite in the eye and he says will it be in the papers? and I say sure, maybe, hard to say I suppose, and I explain how this is really only a courtesy notice for now, that there's no guarantee of anything just yet but that he's in a really strong position, and he takes quick raspy sips of his tea and his eyes darting all across the maps and operational charts and not taking any one bit of it in and I start laughing (puzzled clumsy laughter: this is not how I had expected things to play out) that I try to cover up by saying again how proud he should be, what an honour it is, and he says to me quietly that he didn't really do all that much, you know? that stuff just kind of happened, and I tell him that's ok, that it's just the way these things go sometimes, that we have all the interviews bagged up and he probably just needs to stop giving himself such a rough time about it and this seems to loosen him up a little and he stills his hands on the table edge and he looks me almost straight, almost smiling, and we get to talking about the rest of the process for a minute or two and then he stops me dead like maybe he's heard something or remembered something and he says, but what about the others? and I say the others? and he says what about kyle and marty? and I say look this isn't about what happened, ok, it's about what you did, you need *to remember that, yeah? and his hands start going again and he chews his lips and he leans in, voice lowered, his breath slightly staled, and he says I don't know boss, I don't know if I can do it, and I clamp a big open paw on his shoulder (and I'm thinking, do it? do fucking what?) and it is then I feed him that tired old line about that very attitude of his, that stark and childlike humility, justifying for me the rightness of their commendation, and I hurry him up with his tea and I dismiss him and I shake my head and laugh and I rub the bridge of my nose and I call over and I say hey lofty, did you hear woody there nearly refuse a fucking recommendation for an MC? did you ever hear of any such crackpot lunacy? and we laugh amused paternal laughs about the peculiar ways the lads sometimes have with things, and what the hell did we know; and later, when I have learned a thing or two myself, by total fluke I catch woody picking up his gong on the lunchtime news and he does not give the interviewer his face but speaks to the middle-distance either side of her knees, something about just doing what he had to do (he says it firmly, with a kind of rabbit's foot confidence, like a phrase he has deliberately accustomed himself to), watching his smile thin as she heaps insistent honours upon him, as she refuses him the disavowal of his modesty: hero, she says, hero, hero; and it is then I get it, that I see it like a thing revealed for the first time in a bald unsparing light: that all any of it really amounted to was a game of chance; of people, place and time and an indifferent roll of the dice (and what glory can we justly assert for ourselves when great and terrible acts both should be founded on the intersection of simple accident; will we then also claim authorship of disaster?), and that their accolades in any case were intended not to honour greatness but to palliate their own consciences, their own palsied unquiet beliefs, to conceal from themselves our deep true motives for being there (shit we only ever wanted to fight, that was all of it, all there ever was, and what honest value is accrued when some good and noble thing should chance from out of such shabby impulses?), and finally then that the brash sweeping whitewash of their kindest judgements should also wipe away every small and careful and honest thing that truly was accomplished, and at such awful cost: frail priceless secret things that would not survive even the severity of the words put around them to give them shape (and who would exhange the smallest of these for all the hollow proclamations in the world?); and as we learned from the old wars the dirty lie of pro patria mori, and then of the fraudulence of ideology as a justification for the slaughter of men, I wondered, watching him try to hide his eyes from the cameras, that having done away with those dead religions of country and idea, if it would be hubris or heresy to suppose our legacy as warmakers of a new century would be to make a slur of heroism itself*

They had moved out while it was still dark following the powdered footfall of the man in front, heaving and straining under the weight and their breath coming out in ragged gasps so their tongues stuck in their mouths. The sweat on their foreheads turning cold against the leather helmet inserts. They picked their way waist-high through the spidertrenches and craters, taking light and exaggerated and loping strides over the trip wires pitched taut between the trench walls. You could smell *them* in the dirt. There was the sound of the wind beating through the treeline ahead of them and the slabbed silhouette of the hill rearing blackly at their eight and an oily smear of sky picking out boneshapes of farm buildings in windowless cross-section and scaffolding stripped clean by HE. On the hilltop the major watched the column concertinaing into the darkness, wondering to himself what it was about a diversionary attack that seemed so absurd, why it somehow made it harder to die. The major loved the war very much and these thoughts were like a challenge to his faith. He had spoken to them of fear and of doing your duty to the Corps and to each other and he watched the column fan out into arrowhead as it reached the open ground and it was comforting to imagine each of them, at that moment, thinking silently of their duty. On the approach to the copse the wind had suddenly dropped away leaving a silence in its place that was resonant and full of things unmoving. When the guns opened up Charlie took a round to his face. He was walking around with one hand over his eye saying, boys, boys, I think I got hit, with incoming pulling up the dirt where he stood and one of the corporals trying to scruff him down into the shallow-tilled soil. Charlie was in a bad way. He went quiet quickly, his face bleeding out into the ground. Both sections withdrew into cover amidst the glad moonless ruins of an abandoned wheat silo: rainbow spits of tracer fire crisscrossing out of the darkness and the sound of their own guns singing still in their ears and an afterfeeling that nagged a fivepenny-twopenny pattern at their tails: and it was only out of the killing area, catching breath in that revelatory way, that they realised Charlie and Brady and Cal had been left behind (yeah opal zero uh this is opal two we have uh we have three friendlies down at point of contact, uh heavy direct fire on our position, request immediate support over, immediately). You could see it in their eyes when the realisation kicked in. One of the kids had started crying. Just started bawling into his hands. That was an awful thing to see. The hillside lit up with a piñata burst of muzzleflash from where the sniper teams were snatching off shots in hurried succession to hold back the fighters moving in along the treeline. The major watched them advancing. Figures hot and white and anonymous against the ghostgreen of the night vision. The curious way they would stop, rock once on their heels, and slump forward gently into their kneecaps after a sniper round had emptied the backs of their heads. Industrial smells and gunsmoke washed up off the scree. The interpreter was holding a handset to his ear and dancing where he stood saying, they going to try and take our men alive, sir, they say they have Talib coming west and east, sir they say they going to take them alive sir sir sir (topaz one-nine I want a fire mission in front of that position in seconds few, opal two get some fire support onto that location and get our boys the fuck out of there). Gorman called in a grid for the artillery tight enough to Cal and the others on the exposed forward line for there to be visible overlap on his one-in-fifty. His voice drilled and full of hard edges, a beautiful performance amidst the quickening sense of dread and secret guilty relief stunning his men to open-mouthed dumbness. Childish poses. The distinct crack of gunfire snapped overhead and the plaster burst into flossy clouds on the walltops. Before the 105s hit there was the long sad whistle of the shells, their stomachs dropping away inside of them: Cal lay over Charlie pulling his head tight into his chest: then a moment of serene and absolute silence

: then it was like the earth was coughing them up from its deepest places and the whole horizon went up midday bright, turning the wrinkled terrain into a photo negative of sulphur colours on severe black. Cal took a mouthful of dirt, the first blast turning him on his head and opening him up chin and arms and fists and eyes (check your fire check your fire *jesus christ*), this slow and violent sloshing of his insides. Brady was lying ten feet across the way facedown in a ditch. Gorman walked the 105s back behind the trees until their silhouettes flared black and papery and finely skeletal ahead of the blast light, the shockwaves rolling out on a miss-one-two lag that punched the dust off the walls onto his radio set. Both sections worked their way back across the open ground in slow and scrappy doglegs. The fighting was fiercest out by Three Cigars, with the machine gunners firing from the waist just to get clearance over the scrub and the hollow pop of mortars ringing out one after the other down the line. The fight was four hours old when they reached Brady. He had been killed instantly by a bullet gone into his jaw and up into his helmet. He was white when they got to him. An ignominious contortion they were shamed to look at. They wrapped him in tarpaulin and dragged him by his boots back through the soil, the false falling daylight of illum shells over the enemy bunkers setting the footed struts of their shadows to stretch and spin in leery carnival array. When they finally made Cal he was firing from his pistol, his rifle bayonet-fixed and abandoned at his feet on a pile of emptied magazines and his face streaked black with grease and gunsoot and he was breathing fierce hot sobbing lungfuls as he fired and even as they put themselves under his shoulders, stray rounds pinging overhead and the far-off chug of the medevac Chinook swinging into the patrol base, he sawed at their arms like he meant to go back in alone, his eyes drawn unblinking and jittered and poring fixedly into the long low stand of trees turned once again to stillness and densely thatched shadow, already not really *seeing*, already upon him that rare expression that is a looking through and a looking beyond, that seeks in the outward manifestation of things only the handiwork of apparitions ever-moving and ever-treacherous behind the sleekly curtained veneer. The post-incident report would note that Charlie should have died from the wounds he sustained, excepting the crude compress fashioned out of Cal's own field dressing and the three litres of blood pumped into him by the ERT medics as they taxied into Bastion. Charlie would go on to make a fine recovery, charming the nurses in a clean and well-lit ward in Sellyoak that smelt of bleach and of bedridden body smells and of lilies blooming in the slats of late afternoon sunlight and of butchers' meat and of bad memories. A telltale pink crescent-shaped scar nestled under his left eye. Cal received the MC for his actions that night (for extreme gallantry under fire... his only thoughts were for his colleague, Lance Corporal Newman, as he continued to fight a highly determined and ferocious enemy at close range), a medal he would later pawn on eBay for six grand to pay for his daughter's school uniform in the summer and enough rent and whisky to keep him easy-mannered until December blew in and he wound up getting himself arrested for actual outside a convenience store in Cardiff. The day after the attack the major had sat out on the hilltop watching the smoke from the bunkers drifting up trim and crisply piped against the early morning haze. It's the fat, someone had said. It takes a long time to burn. The morning was bright and cold. There were the perfumed smells of the sand blowing up out of the swale and the morning light pooling the blueshadowed folds in the far hills and the certainty of the morning made the sordid and terrible things in the night seem like an untruth. Afghan policemen were squatted down by the gun positions looking to score brass for onsale. Word from command was that Juliet Company had taken the main objective at Jugroom.

up out of the ditch with my shoulders high to my ears and my breathing coming hard like I might have taken a sly sucker to the stomach, the men shake out into an extended line either side of me and we advance flatly across the field to the far woodline, bonzo hissing over our headsets to steady the formation, he metes each footstep out left and right and I am glad for this, glad that it should be gruff and direct and unapologetic and that it should absolve me of any deliberation over the very sense and soundness underpinning those individual strides (and we all get to know this eventually, how even the most violent swells of instinct or conscience can be overcome if they are resolved to an accumulation of single steps), and we are hunched in on ourselves like peasant women, straining the distant undergrowth for muzzleflash or some telltale snicker of smoke or the crack and whee of a bullet seeking out the ready softness of our skulls, dead man's click underboot, steady now, keep her steady lads, left right, and each step is an anticipation, each step is taken heavy-legged, muscles pinched and hard, crystalled sweat like wool glass breaking the skin, the crunch of woodchip and stone underfoot in the soft doughy soil twanging wires that ring up reflexively through a tautness of nerve and sinew, we set the dry powdered dirt whirling and it clings to us like sugar icing and bonzo is turned shoulder-on slightly to the axis of advance and his face kind of wincing and scrunched up like he might be expecting an errant cricket ball from short and he catches me looking over and he strains a grin, steady he says, left right left right, and the uniform tick of his voice finds a deeper resonance: uncountable hours of parade square drilling to bring to harness by degrees the wild raw power of instinct, to heel that rebellious nature that would shy at the command to march like dumb fucking tommies across open ground to some posited enemy gunline, a nature not of childlike faith in those men appointed to positions of power but ever one of mistrust and second-guessing, a nature inclined to scrutinise the necessity of every order, unable to

103

blinker itself to the quiet insistence of its doubting (and this is where instinct most closely resembles conscience, where the personal is impinged by the violences of duty, and those that act upon it are garlanded or they are put up against the wall); and we hit the woodline like an exhalation, boots and muzzles to tramp back the thick standing elephant grass, to chase out the shadows and fall like infants into the motherly arms of our own relief; and some time later I am crossing the raked gravelbed between the dhobi store and the ops tent and whistling to myself and I abrupt mid-stride: left boot out in front of me, halted, dangled, my body stiff in that acuteness that prefigures fight or flight, fuck up or fuck off: something in the arrangement of stones that triggers whole entire systems of reflex and response: my breath quickened like I've taken a sucker to the stomach and a sudden prickling collar sweat and my muscles explosively balled: some cipher in that random and unremarkable spread of stones that intercedes directly with my unbidden unconscious self to warn that I will surely die if I take that next step: that my legs should obliterate below the knee and I will be razed instantly of feature and prominence like a scrap of bald scorched earth, tumbled raggedly skyward, and I am rooted there dumbly until a passing shadow revives me to myself like a splash of cold sinkwater; and what did we think would happen, comandeering those ancient associations of stimuli and instinct that we might subdue the beast that roams, that we might recruit them in defection instead as instruments of order and discipline, that it would be like rewiring a fucking fuse? that it wouldn't somehow undermine everything firm and certain and sound?

In the evening they talk and smoke and administer themselves in huddles while the sentries take up their points in overwatch. The daylight is dying away to a thin, fierce glacial light that does strange things to the shadows and the desertfloor colours. Sky clear and starless. There are four of them. They are three of them bearded and one other, a week unshaven, sat back slightly from the group affecting the peculiar open-legged sprawl characteristic of marines that have fought plenty and sat about plenty. They are war-coloured. The sand greenly coarse in their hair and skin and undernail and about them there is a smell that is fetid and sweatsour and not entirely unpleasant. A sweetness of deep moist earth. At short remove they have the look of storybook hobos riding out another day belly-empty and penny-poor.

– I got one for you, says Jonas.

He turns his face to his hands and lights his smoke and he shakes the match dry. One of a vanishing romantic few to still use matches in the field despite their ludicrous impracticality.

– Heard it from this yank I got chatting to on our way through Bastion.

They are swapping stories. *Spinning dits.* It is a kind of sport and it was a way to pass the time and it is a way to talk when there is no way to talk. This is something the new guy has learned.

– This ought to be good, says Angry.

Garrett and Angry swap quick coded glances that go unseen under Jonas's loose hands, under the swell of his chatter. Garrett settles back onto his elbows. An emperor's pose. He wears a tatty old roachbitten pilgrim blanket and his hair is stiff with dust and he carries the heaviness of his beard already below the jawline, giving him this look of red-eyed vagrancy in excess even of the regular squalor that attends long-range patrolling.

– Come on then, he says. Let's have it.

Talk had earlier started on the Taliban sniper who made his living in those parts: three of them passing comment between mouthfuls of sausage 'n beans forked out of boiling foil pouches, the new guy out at the edges observing a carefully-toed line in attentive inoffensive quiet. This had seemed as good a start as any since all anyone really knew about the sniper was rumour and gossipy scraps, much of it conflicting, occultly dark, and like the very best dit-spinning this gave them license to extrapolate and invent with maximal heel space. It was a good start too because the sniper was locally famed for his craft, stories or no, and this gave an added weight, an urgency, to the telling: the new guy had felt something cold wriggle between his shoulderblades when they spoke of the two soldiers thought to have been felled by a single well-conceived well-articulated bullet. The night is smoothing in now on a glassy shoal of sky and the regretful sound of the wind worries deep in the valley and the telling has assumed something of the cosy horror of stories recounted by campfire. Enough to send you shivers in your tail and to turn day-truths into childishness. Like they might somehow just be makebelieve after all.

– So this yank I was chatting to, he was the real American deal. The full cheeseburger. You know the sort. He was chewing baccie and spitting up in this gopping screwtop tin he carried with him and he was sporting a full forearm of them God-bothering wristbands. So I can't make any call on his authenticity. But this yank, right, he told me he was Force Recon intelligence, and he reckoned that our sniper friend had been bobbing back and forth between CIA and SOCOM kill lists for coming on eight years before he showed up here in the valley.

– That right? says Angry.

Jonas nods.

– Eight years? Huh.

The new guy studies Jonas in covert glances. He wears his body armour over bare tattooed arms under his open jacket, a sweatrag bound and tied on each wrist, his cigarettes pocketed visibly over his zap number and blood group annotated in bolded two-inch flattip marker pen. Like some sort of mixed homage to tropes of war movies past. He is brightly animated when he speaks and his eyes seek out first Garrett and then Angry on alternate passes, neither of whom seem to hold his stare for anything more than maybe a second or two at a time. Jonas's chat has this evangelical edge to it. It lends him an easy talky charm and it makes you believe him with your deep body instincts even while your head is busy taking it all to pieces.

– Get this. Apparently our guy used to be just some yokel farmer out in Chechnya. Lived there with his family out in the sticks years back. I mean, the guy's not even a genuine fucking sandnigger! – Turning his hands out to Garrett and Angry, laughing through his nostrils – Right. So we've got this yokel Chechen kid that splits his days working the fields or driving all the turnips and shit into town. (How the fuck am I supposed to know what they farm? Give me a break, Gats). That's the way of it for a long time. Then the nineties roll round. The Ruskies invade.

Pause. The steal of a smile up over his teeth.

– This one winter a Russian troop marches into the family farmstead while he's out doing his rounds. They burn the fucker down. Execute the lot of them up against the barn walls. That's how he finds them. All shot up to shit against the barn. It turns him crazy, like it would. And this kid, instead of cutting his losses and hauling arse and turnip to the nearest taverna and thanking heartily whichever deity it is he's got working comms with for sparing him, this kid he starts *stalking* the Russians back through the hills. Fucking stalking them. And one by one he slots them as they march. He teaches himself to shoot and to track the poor bastards by their sign and to use the forests to hit them and melt away again. Teaches himself all of it from a standing start, figuring it out piece on piece as he goes. And the thing is, the really *fucked up* part, right, he starts getting this taste for shooting the bollocks off them while they're still alive. He likes to kill them slow and deliberate with four or five carefully placed body shots before he goes in to collect the goods, rusty khukri fully unsheathed. By the time he's worked his way down to the last ten or so they aren't even trying to take their dead buddies with them anymore. He's got them so fucking scared they're not even returning fire except to flee and scatter, and out he descends from the wooded hilltops to claim whatever's left of their nuts as a souvenir. Only one of the Russians ever made it back to the company outpost. He'd been neutered too.

Jonas takes a drag on his cigarette. Cool theatric precision. They smoke with habitual stealth, each of them, tab between thumb and forefinger and the stubend directed into the heel of their palms to hide the telltale cherry glow, the smoke fed out faintly against their cheeks. It is one of those rare strange things that the war seems unable to spoil. Calming and tender. It kills the sick feeling always inside of them. The new guy has found he can chain an easy four or five out on patrol without getting that hammerblow lobal nicotine hit. Hard living being a matter of such small consolations.

Jonas turns out and hocks one off and turns in.

— So anyway, his fame gets ahead of him. Al Qaeda starts taking notice. This Force Recon guy reckons he even got a meet-and-greet with bin Laden himself back before nine eleven. Course, those AQ boys did a good job turning him into one mean bitter muslim motherfuck. Got him believing the infidel yanks were tied up in some sort of holy crusade in the Ganners. And so they pack him off to one of them training camps in Pakistan, right, where they have him mentoring whole schools of baby jihadists shipping across the border. And then, probably only a year or two ago now, they moved him up the wire with a single mission that he was there to see through or die trying: to shoot the bollocks off every single British soldier in the Sangin Valley.

The four of them go quiet as he finishes. You can hear the night whipping in between the wagons parked up on the summit.

– Is that… true? the new guy says.

They break into low and mucky laughter.

– Don't be fucking simple, says Jonas.

This is another thing to learn about the stories: there is truth to them sure enough, but you only ever find it in the unlikely places. Rarely where it announces itself.

Garrett is flossing and squinting at a hazed plastic handmirror balanced on one knee. Angry is absently squeezing and wringing an empty plastic water bottle like an accordion, his forearms thickening and bunching and tattooblue to the knuckle. The bottle spidered white with plastic stress fractures. Watching Angry from where he is sat, softed some in evening gloom, the new guy can't shake this image of an over-developed child hunched roundly on his toys, bludgeoning his shapes and holes.

– So how come, says Angry, how come if this fucker's had the CIA or Seal Team Six or whothefuckever all over his mirrors for the last eight years, then how come nobody's managed to bag him? How come he ain't kitted out in an orange boilersuit and getting the wet flannel treatment daily from Uncle Sam?

– That's the beauty of it. This guy doesn't have any connections, any history here, and he does his work alone. No friends. No family. No mobiles or emails or meetings. No sloppy COMSEC to catch him out. And cos he's got this whole bollock-shooting thing going he doesn't even need to touch in with his raghead handler in Pakistan for tasking. The whole mad grizzly enterprise just kind of runs off its own juice. – Grinding his tab out underheel, letting the last of it cloud deliciously between tongue and palate – And so this Force Recon guy was saying the problem is they basically can't catch a lucky break with the fucker. There's no one anywhere near close enough to squeal on his movements and there aren't any texts or emails flying around to get a hot fix on where he is. They're always playing catch-up. Always chasing down this perpetually half-cold trail of neutered Afghans and distance-headshots that would probably raise a few admiring eyebrows from our own very brightest and very sharpest of shooters.

– I don't buy it, says Angry.

Garrett is inspecting his dental floss for finds against a dull evening backlight. He wipes it clean on the thigh of one trouserleg and begins work on his bottom jaw.

– That ain't what I heard, says Angry.

– Oh yeah? says Jonas.

– I was talkin to Buster from BRF about this like only two or three days ago. He had a whole different take on it.

– Oh yeah?

– Yeah.

The bottle makes a cracking noise in Angry's hands, the plastic suddenly broken open along the spiral-seam of the twist. He looks it with surprise. Wrenches both ends until the break shears the bottle into jagged halves that he plops, abandoned, disinterested, between his boots. Angry is said to be a little tapped in the head, although there is disagreement as to how he had come to be this way (this had been told the new guy on joining the troop as a kind of instructional gizzit between signing out his morphine and an environmental hazards lecturette). Some claimed the fighting had nudged his wiring loose. Others said he had always been crazier than a boxful of ferrets and this was just him gone fully native. It was mostly academic though: you don't get a name like Angry in the marines lightly.

– Buster reckons this guy has his shit nailed down for sure. I mean, he was gobbing off a bit. Giving it the big one and all. You know Buster. But he sounded pretty clued up. Those BRF boys get to see a thing or two on their travels.

– Yeah and don't we fucking know about it, says Jonas.

Angry lights himself a tab. Broad fingers swallowing the tiny stub of roach. He slows himself visibly, like a four-tonner shunting through its gears. Not showing any hurry to continue this particular line but taking these deep contemplative lungfuls that give up clear and billowed in the coldness. He raises his head and looks out over the valley. An inversion, almost, of twilight's configuring, with crisp starlight studding now the highest instep of sky above them and the sky the deepness and colouring and gradation of ocean trenches, bent way out into distant hills peaked still with a fine whitely watery daylight. Down in the blackness of the valley the wind moves like an animal in a cage.

– So what was Buster's take? says Garrett, through floss and tongue and cram of fingers.

– Buster? He was basically saying this fucker has his shit in one sock. That he's properly squared himself away on his drills and tradecraft. He's sposed to have recruited an army of thirty or forty dickers that he's using for target spotting and close protection. Loads of kids. Some farmers, some shopkeepers. Banditos on motorbikes. The usual Terry jumblesale entourage. And he was saying they've been keeping eyes on these dickers from up in the hides for a while now. Saying they're basically this network of like, shit, I dunno, *feelers* he's got creeping out across three-odd square miles of the frontline. Like you've got each of these dickers doing their own individual thing, but somehow it all comes together as a kind of smart working whole. Like how an ant nest does its business. It means he knows where we are and where we're going almost the moment we put a boot out of camp. That makes him hard to find and it makes him hard to kill and it makes him one dangerous Talib to fuck with.

– And how exactly is BRF meant to have worked all *that* out? says Jonas.

– Dunno. – Shrugging – That's their job, ain't it? Watching. Waiting. Spose if you ping a kid sendin a text from his pushbike in one minute and in the next you've got some poor Afghan rozzer fillin his brains into his helmet then you just put two and two together.

– Huh. Sounds like a lot of fucking guesswork to me.

– Maybe. Angry shrugs. He does not look like contesting the point.

The new guy has already once seen Angry at work. The performance had had that unmistakable quality of greatness immediately apparent to layman and connoisseur alike. A sensation of witnessing something outside time. His was this rare sheer talent for soldiering that gave the disquieting feeling of Angry having very definitely and very pointedly been put together for that singular living purpose. The talent in this instance being his emotional detachment, and his consequent ability to fight with extraordinary ferocity whilst maintaining near-sorporific levels of calm (manifesting itself as wry disdain and a general steady low-level state of disgust), meaning he is almost incalculably valuable to his troop and unit (both in terms of soldierly utility and talismanic morale); more likely to be killed by a probable ratio of half again (the cruel weighting of the odds against the brave, the stupid, and the professionally competent, at least two categories of which he is almost certain to occupy at any one time); and almost genetically hardcoded to fail at anything that falls outside the narrow heights of his genius. As if you might divine in the coolly unselfconscious way he looks out now on the purpled darkening plains, in the effortless, almost masterful tranquility with which he rocks into heel and haunch, the butterflyflap of a suicide many years and disasters still adrift.

– I'm calling Buster out on this one, says Jonas. There's no way this guy has made it eight fucking years on a US kill list with however-many dickers it is he's got flying about the place sending out bungloads of phonecalls and radio intercept and satellite comms and Skype and SM-fucking-S. You can barely switch on a fucking headtorch around here without a Predator spinning up its entire Hellfire battery.

Angry shrugs. Sends his spent tab pinwheeling towards the drop with a practised palm down thumb-and-finger flick, sparks of ash and coal lofted into the darkness by a black snuff of wind.

– I never said nothing about no kill list. That was all you.

– I'm just telling you what I heard, says Jonas. And if it gets to calling things between US intelligence and your bezzie mate Buster Brown from BRF, then I reckon I have a decent idea which side of the shitter I'm falling on.

Garrett has his toothbrush up at a three-quarter pitch to hit his back teeth, his mouth foaming. He stops at this. Huffs. Spits, slinging the foam off into the dirt.

– Sounds to me, Jones, he says, like you've got a bit of a lob-on for this sniper bloke.

Angry laughs.

– What's that supposed to mean? says Jonas.

Pause.

– Nothing.

– No, go on. Tell me.

– Nothing. I didn't mean nothing by it.

– Go on. What's that supposed to mean, about me having a hard-on or whatever?

– *Lob-on*, says Angry. A wicked spread grin.

Garrett spits and then rinses and then spits, wipes his mouth clean from elbow to cuff. The effect is peculiar, revealing the immaculate white-yellow glisten of his teeth on dark and dusty leatherhide skin. Garrett is twenty-three and already section commander. He looks impossibly old. Bowed, almost crooked-shouldered. The new guy can't imagine him having ever not been out there in the desert. Ever cleanskinned and soft-haired and wholesomely upstood, ever not carrying the war like a devil on his back. Garrett pockets the toothbrush and he pulls that old woollen blanket tight in over his shoulders and the new guy catches him sneaking Angry this dirty mischief smile that is at once a hands-high admission of guilt, *Busted!*, and a statement of outright intent: fuck it: in for a penny, in for a pound.

– Look, mate, Jones, you do talk some serious fucking chod sometimes.

Garrett puts an open smile on it and throws his palms out at Jonas, appealing to the three of them with highshrugged shoulders and doe eyes and this *well someone had to say it* pouted bottom lip. Frankness always a fine trojan for bile. Jonas has this uncomfortable fidgety look like he doesn't know where to put his eyes.

– And what's with all this bollock-shooting mass-murder stuff anyway? Christ. Like things aren't fucked up enough exactly the way they are. That stuff might go down a bomb with your civvie mates and all. Some gullible chick you're trying to bag off or whatever. Fair one. But it's getting a bit fucking… tired. Yeah?

Jonas sits there, breaking rocks with his heels.

– Just give it a rest. Yeah? That's all I'm saying.

The new guy shifts in his seat. Keeps himself strictly neutral in posture and gaze, instinctively sensing danger in the shifting pack dynamics. Knowing with boyhood reflexes about how wounded pride likes to revenge itself on smaller creatures, about how his simply being there, simply standing witness, is reason sufficient to call down a whole storm of vengeance. Keep quiet and keep shut the fuck up. That's what they had told him before he left. And this is something else to the stories too. Something secret and cardinal and hard to learn. Something about entitlement, and about the stories only truly belonging to those that hate the war. Something about the stories revealing your heart.

Jonas drags his heel under his knee and back out again a couple of times, describing a straight shallow line in the dirt. Chews his lips.

– Whatever. I'm just telling you what I heard.

Up on the point the first sentries are being swapped. There are the rustling shuffling sounds of others taking to their slugs. Angry and the new guy throw on duffel jackets and chunkyknit woollen hats. Their fingertips chap with memories of old moorland frostnip. It is a desert cold that doesn't give shape to their breath but clings like jellied gasoline to their insides, seems to chill them outwardly from their bonemarrow. The quiet between them is embarrassed and ungainly and slow-moving. It catches on all their little noises, announcing itself like the creep of a well-intentioned drunk through a sleeping house.

– Ok, says Garrett. Gather round children. I've got a dit for you.

He looks to the three of them in turn, though the new guy understands it automatically as a gesture to Jonas alone. Deniable, imprecise. Heaped under performance and a throwaway smile. But a gesture nonetheless. And it is strange that gestures should carry such weight in a place where sorries are the very smallest of currencies.

– You'll like this. Here, Angry, chuck us one of those mucker.

Angry shakes out his tabs and they draw one each. They light them into cupped hands, the undersides of their cheeks and eyelids flared briefly over their fingertips as if by a click of torchlight. Garrett puts the smoke off to one side and he looks the three of them again in turn, slowly, bent forward over crossed legs, the blanket pulled high on his neck.

– You've got to hear me out on something first though.

Pause.

– What I've got, the story…the terp told me it.

He grins, watches this settle. Angry laughs.

– Fuck *off*, says Jonas.

– I'm serious.

– *Fuck off*. Pacman? Seriously?

– Uh huh.

– You're the one picking *me* up for talking chod and you're gonna go believe fucking *Pacman* over my Force Recon guy?

– Ok, ok. – Holding his palms high – Like I said, hear me out first. Give me a chance. Besides, the way I see it, when you've got a yank spinning you a dit nine times out of ten he's really only trying to tell you what a fucking big shot he is anyway. Force Recon or whatever. Big fucking whoop. At least with the Afghans you know you're getting treated to a pucker porterhouse-sized slab of story.

Jonas sucks his lips in and shakes his head. Pacman, he mutters. Well holy fuck.

– Come on then Gats, says Angry. Don't leave us dangling.

– So apparently it's kind of a folk story around here. But the terp swears blind there's something to it. That he knows a guy who knows a guy who knows a guy who can verify. Funny that, huh?

He massages his fists one after the other. Palm and knuckles making a dry papery sound.

– So the dit goes that there were these two Pashtun brothers who grew up in a town somewhere up north. Oruzgan, I think. Their dad is supposed to have trained them up as crackshots from when they were only kneehigh to a gnat, each of them given their own personal Dragunov that the dad customises and tinkers with to match their little growing bodies. And soon enough these kids have earned a sort of name for themselves around town for their sharpshooting. Protecting the livestock from the wild animals that come out of the mountains during the hard seasons. Scaring off the bandits that wander the town's outer limits. That sort of stuff. Now these two brothers had been crazy competitive their whole lives and, sure as anything, sure as shit, they get a hair or two on their ballsacks and end up, both of them, falling arse-over-tit for this pretty young thing in the town. The whole thing quickly turning ratshit to jealousy and paranoia and stupid angry spoken things they can't take back, and then to this feud between them that splits the township smartly down the middle, forcing the elders to settle things by competition: a shootout over some lunatic distance, the loser of which is subject to exile. Banishment. The long walk. Now the night before the shoot, one brother does the unthinkable. He perverts the one sacred rule they live by, the one untouchable thing between them: and he nudges his brother's sights off-centre. On the day of the competition this first brother steps up and bangs out a perfect set. Doesn't break sweat. A clean ten-out-of-ten. Then the elders instruct the pretty little object of the boys' affections to run on out and switch targets for the next shoot. Can you see where this is headed? The second brother lines up his shot and he settles his breathing and he gets that coin of light sitting just right in his scope and he takes his opening shot and he kills the girl where she stands, a full twenty-feet right of the target.

Garrett lets this hang, looking back over his shoulder to itch his neck. He turns out again.

– This first brother, messed up with guilt and remorse, he escapes out into the desert where he becomes a crooked gun for hire. Selling his time and brass to the highest bidder and settling up a whole slew of dirty old scores along the way.

– And this guy is meant to be our sniper? says Jonas. Some lovesick idiot on the hoof?

– You're getting ahead of me. This is where it gets good. See, at this point in almost any other story you'd expect a run-in with the other brother, right? A showdown maybe. Something to tie up all the loose threads, pull it together into a tidy little bundle. But Pashtun dit-spinning is better than that. It's *above* all that. It doesn't give a dry fuck about a satisyfing ending or any kind of logical progression of the story. It just seems to kind of bimble off on whatever bonkers tangent first takes its fancy. I like that. It seems, I don't know, more... more honest somehow. So what happens is this: the Taliban get wind of this freelance gunslinger who's kept himself occupied knocking off various high-profile dealers and politicians and gangsters, and so they send out an emissary to test his skills. This emissary asks the sniper to shoot the bell from the neck of a goat at three hundred paces. Now this would be a piece of piss normally, but it's a redders summer's day, the kind where you've got the heat moving everything in shimmers. The brother snaps the rifle to his shoulder and fires, *blam*. Nothing happens. The emissary shakes his head, his entourage collapsing in laughter.

The brother only shrugs. When they go to inspect more closely they find that he has shot out the clapper without setting the bell off. *Without even startling the fucking goat.* Sure, he turns out to be a fine investment: he is hated and hateful and more handy with a seven-six-two than just about any other man to ever put on a grubby dishdash and a pair of flip-flops. Gracious enough to embrace sharia too for the shitloads of bullion they wheelbarrow his way. The end. Roll credits.

Pause.

– That's it? says Jonas.

– That's it.

– What a load of horseshit.

– More horseshit than your bollock-shooting ghost?

– Psht. Way to go Pacman, the dumb yokel fuck. You can tell him I said that.

– I'll be sure to.

The story has warmed them. They seem at ease again with each other, limber. Jonas has lost that wincing hunted expression. Angry is spread out on the dirt with his boots crossed and his arms under his head and his duffel jacket zipped flush to his throat and his eyelids opening and closing in heavy sated swoops. You can somehow tell the sentry points off in the darkness by their silence, conspicuous like a held breath. The wind sounds in the valley. Pathetic and persistent, blustering like a lost child, empty now of the menace that freighted it. There is a sudden good feeling, and of that feeling being impermanent and soon to be lost and precious because of that impermanence, and of wanting to hold onto that feeling.

The new guy checks his watch and sees he is due a shift on the point in ten. He rubs his eyeballs with thumb and forefinger. Drags his fingers crackling through stubbled cheeks. He checks off his gear where he is sat and begins packing his daysack in a meticulous, ordered routine. He is still in that first bloom of conscientiousness for his work, wholly unskeptical, a true believer, and the others look on this as a novelty and an amusement, like old sweat inmates sweetly admiring a first-timer and the regular letters to his girl back home, unable to recall a time when the war for them too seemed a fantastical and overwrought imitation of its real self.

– What about you? says Garrett, scooting a sudden quarter-turn towards him. What's your take on this guy?

Jonas looks over. Angry flexes one leg at the knee to fart and rolls on his side, settling onto an elbow and squinting. The whites of their eyes in the darkness fixing him where he sits.

– What do you reckon?

The new guy pauses before replying, his cheeks hot. Flattered, stupidly, by their attention and ashamed too at such easy flattery. The unexpectedness of their attention on him heavy like a bowling ball in the lap.

His tongue probes for words, rolls them around a little in his mouth. But nothing comes right or true. And he feels himself suddenly without history, without the necessary things to say to give him substance. Adrift and formless as though waking into blackness in an unfamiliar room. And he understands then, for the first time, how the stories are also a kind of building, a joining together of discarded things. A spark wrought from dead hopeless pieces. From snipers, from careless dinnertalk, from memories traded over an open flame. A way yet to save something whole from a richness of loss.

The sky is transfigured now to starlight, the birthmark smear of galaxies giving their gentle coloured light to the hills, and the new guy shuffles his boots out into that open-legged sprawl he has seen and he blows his fists and rubs his hands and he glances out over the valley and he sucks it down into his lungs and he says to them, well, he says, well. Get this.

we put down in kandahar airfield overnight in early june and the next day we walk the long ploughed roads with the buses running circuits and a broad wind rattling the roadside chainlink, and we wander wrapped in roughly napped woollen blankets, hair and beards stuck fast and our eyes ice-white pools set on skin the colour of stone, soldiers and contractors eyeing us from a distance, and we order sloppy quarter pounders and fries and coke and milkshakes from the takeout along the arcade and we cherish them and eat them where we stand, a childish dismay at the leftovers we have to pitch as it balloons half-chewed in our shrunken stomachs, staggering joint to joint, jonas puking a gutload of vanilla and cream frappuccino onto the decking and this canadian officer looking him boot to bumper and issuing a curt verdict: young man, you should be rightly ashamed of yourself: and the next thing they're unpeeling my fists from his fucking collar, talking me back from some distant place that reveals itself to me sudden and vivid and whole, it's not worth it boss, laughter, back slapping, and in the afternoon we sleep dead sleep and in the evening we eat in the dining hall: table on table, soldiers talking loudly and laughing and clattering trays under the thin dazzle of generator lamps, and we sit hunkered in the cosy gloom of half-finished sentences and grunts and expressions only lazily formed: we, us, them; and someone leans across and asks if we are heading over to the nightclub later and I watch garrett bunch up his eyes under his brow and think about this and then he asks, slowly, they have a nightclub here? and he looks back down at the table and shakes his head in a way that expresses confusion and disgust and a sense of suddenly finding oneself unable to explain the machinations of worldly things

Haji Musa Khan was a crook and a murderer and a mean-looking old bastard and I couldn't help but like him. He spoke with an amused and silent condescension that gave you this feeling everything he said had a smile buried beneath it. He spoke slowly and chose his words with care and caught you direct in the eye as though you understood it all plainly. And sometimes he would let that smile steal across his face as the interpreter played his words back in broken English, as if their translation somehow gave them permanence and authority. It wasn't easy to reconcile the man with the monster. But the way his presence disturbed the natural hierarchy in the room spoke of deeper things. Like the play of water on the site of a wreck.

He says how long have you been in Afghanistan?

Long enough, I replied. Khan let out a roar and banged the table.

And he says how long have you been a spy?

I smiled. Would you tell Mr Khan that much as I'd like to spend the day discussing pleasantries, we have pressing issues that need to be dealt with. Issues of mutual interest. As a matter of urgency.

I'm sorry sir, could you repeat that?

Can you tell Mr Khan we need to talk business. Please.

Khan nodded at the interpreter and leaned in towards me, his arms folded and flat against the table, his eyes suddenly shining and hard and the unseen smile all gone from behind them.

He says *so talk*.

We've been caught with our fucking pants down gentlemen, the colonel had said. His voice was all shadows. There was a wall-size map of the province pinned up with HOLD and SCREEN and ENGAGE and HOLD mission verbs scrawled in blue across the belly with arrows coming off them in spokes and innocuous little red boxes that were supposed to represent concentrations of enemy even though you might as well have been trying to hold sand between your fingers. They called it the bear pit. G5 and G3 looked very small in their seats. Knees together and their palms pressed flat to their thighs like schoolboys. The colonel marched the room in big rooster strides and the scent of blood in his nostrils and G5 and G3 sinking further into the chairs on each pass. There was the smell of stale sweat. It reminded me of the Corps boxing when you were watching a light-heavy with three fights already under his belt up against a novice and there was an expectation of violence that was heavy in the air and it made you excited and horrified at your own excitement.

If you HOLD here – the colonel jabbing at the map – you leave yourself exposed here – jab – and here – jab – and you open up infiltration routes all across this northern flank. – jabjabjabjabjab – That's not isolating the enemy. That's a cosmetic re-fucken-calibration of land forces. Am I right? Can someone explain to me exactly why we're *not* going to HOLD here and what we're going to do instead to avoid getting rimmed while we have our collective haunches raised and presented to the elements?

Pause.

I suggest you have a very serious rethink. I'll be back in an hour.

Outside. The sickly light from the ops tent flapped onto us through the canvas openings. The night was cold and very clear. We drank it down into our lungs, felt the cool coming off the rocks beneath our boots. The colonel was drinking out of a 15oz thermos. One hand on his hips and his eyes moving quickly all over the place. And the rest of him so still and calm and poised that you knew skin-down he had to be completely wired. He was very far into character. It made me nervous.

He was speaking at me: It's a game changer, make no mistake.

126

We spent so long trying to stem the tide down south that we barely noticed those desert roaches waltzing in and setting up shop while we had our backs turned. Sweet Mary. All that blood and treasure. Five months and we've only just stumbled onto the vipers' nest right at our very feet.

He was quiet for a moment, stood squarely into a tepid stripe of tentlight.

He told me the Brigadier wanted the offensive to be Afghan-led from the outset. That there would be a company of our marines in support. He had asked what he could expect from my side, and I had said to him that it was difficult to say really, that funding had been suspended and that we were running on goodwill and a whole lot of luck, and he had looked stern and distracted out into the night that was glassy from the cold, and he had said just do what you need to do, and he had finally looked over and he had said mark my words, we will rout these fuckers and we will hit them so hard they won't even dare whisper the word Babaji except in the most abject and solemn tones of reverential fucking awe.

Back then we had outposts scattered across the province and down into the frontiers. The idea had been to hold a secure belt across the centre to stabilise the political elements of the counterinsurgency. People talked a lot about a political solution. Those two words were a totem for diplomats who couldn't stomach the warfighting or who loved the warfighting too much and salved their consciences on a diet of free elections and women's rights and education.

Only the outposts had become isolated and the supply lines had folded. The soldiers in the platoon houses were eating out of their beltkits and fighting to their last bullets with the resup helicopters pulling away under the weight of fire outside. The rotors chopping up the mortar smoke into cobwebs. At the time a Yank major had told me, you boys keep pokin around for trouble and gettin your fingers chewed, and he had looked thoughtful and we had watched the paling sky turn the mountains ahead of us into whispers and sunlight and he had said, things will need to change and many men will need to die 'fo we see the end of this. And it had sounded both prophetic and meaningless as every grand statement had sounded during those long months.

And he says your progress is too slow and that you British are afraid to fight. He says that there is an old Russian proverb that when you are troubled by a single ant you must be ready to pour boiling water on the nest. And he fingered his prayer beads so they made a clacking noise like bone on bone and I looked and I saw the string beaded thickly with tarsals of yellowed bone that played to the intimacies of his fingertips and when I looked to him again he showed a cobbled spread of teeth, his tongue mashing against the gaps.

We might have held the killing fields at Naw Zad and Musa Qala and Sangin but the Taliban and the warlords had carved up everything in between. Khan ruled a fiefdom that reached up through the Marjah flatlands and into the central districts where the elephant grass grew thick and green and stern along the flanks of the river.

Khan's empire was built on pragmatism, drug money and outright brutality. During the opium harvest he gathered the village elders and demanded zakat to protect their fields and he formed militias that laid siege to the poppy eradication forces, driving them with military precision onto the outlying arable land where the farmers were simply too poor to come up with the payments. Columns of shining red tractors turned into ruined hulks at the roadside. Poppy fields churned inside-out, their roots stuck up blinking into the sun. At the end of the harvest we would find severed hands and feet wrapped up in plastic rainwater sheets at the roadside as a warning against other recently out-of-work fighters hoping to run a sideline extorting taxes on Khan's patch. He liked to collect ears. Or so they said.

He says why should he help you?

You are a friend to us. A friend to the British and a friend to the Pashtun. And you are my brother. That is why I have called you here today. As a brother and as a friend. Willing to do what needs to be done.

The interpreter relayed my words with verve and deep intonation and wild gesturing so that they no longer seemed to belong to me. Khan was still. Then he sneered and brushed the remark away.

He says you talk business in one moment and friendship in the next. He asks if you mean to dishonour him by speaking this way.

There is no dishonour in what we ask. You must tell him this. You must be very clear. – Glancing over at the interpreter already sweating his underarms through to black – We invite you here firstly as the leader of your people. We are facing an enemy in strength and numbers the likes of which we have never seen before. He is not your Pashtun brother. He is Pakistani. He is Saudi and he is Chechnyan and he is Bosnian and he is Somali. He is a foreign fighter who only cares about bringing jihad and violence and unrest to the province. This isn't a problem for the British. We will be home soon and there will be many more who will come and who will go and who will forget this place as if it never was. This is a problem for the elders. For the farmers. For the tradesmen and for the workers in the city and for your way of life. This is why we come to you firstly as a friend and as a brother and ask you to join us and do what must be done.

The interpreter quickened as I allowed him to catch up, his voice pitching and breaking.

This is why we come to you as friends and brothers. And ask you to do what must be done.

Again. Deliberate. Slower. Khan watched me closely and then gestured for me to continue.

You are a wise man. You know Marjah will never be the same if these blasphemers ever get a firm foothold in the province. You may be able to reach some sort of agreement with the Pashtun fighters. We understand that. It is sabat. But the foreigners are not interested in your money or your land or your influence or pashtunwali.

Pause.

Do you think the chief of police will favour you once they hold Route 611 and the MSR? When they threaten to murder his wife and children? You'll be cut off. Nothing between you and Baram Chah. Your shipments will dry up. And they will come for you.

Pause.

This is why I appeal to you also as a businessman and a politician. I am only speaking secrets you already hold to be truth. You know all this. And you know you stand to lose everything.

Pause.

You're asking yourself why you should help us? On the contrary, and with all due respect, perhaps you should consider why *we* would want to help *you*.

After the interpreter had finished there was a length of silence that was empty and light and his eyes were glass. I felt a snakeslither of nausea in my bowels. I wondered if I had misjudged the situation. If I had misjudged Khan, and made a miscalculation beyond all mending. And it was only in this sudden understanding that the full heaviness of my task really came upon me for the first time and the words blood and treasure rattled in my skull and I saw the coming battle very clearly.

The halgoen bulbs overhead buzzed in their casings.

Finally, Khan snapped his head back and laughed. He banged the table and dismissed the interpreter from the room to fetch some water. He leant towards me so that I could smell the sweetmeat of decay on his breath, his forearms and fingertips making an A frame in front of him.

Sweet Mary. All that blood and treasure.

Spring brought the snowwater and the fighters down from the mountains and it was during that time that our first patrols reached Nawa and then the southernmost rim of Nad-e Ali where the salt on the furrowed land came up like blanket frost and the bombs by the roadside turned the fighting bitter and ugly and slow. It was late March by the time we had a foothold in Marjah. Marjah was drugs territory. Travelling through the bazaar you would see bin liners fat with opium heaped up in the back rooms. That was the first time I met Khan. He was sat out on the roof of the old police headquarters under a cold blade of sky with two boys squatted at his heels. The boys were all bright eyes and light skin and their hair and nails fired copper red from the henna. I watched his men leaning over the parapet so they could shoot at the dogs scavenging the wasteground out back. They shot recklessly and without discipline and they took great joy when they managed to blow the legs out from one so that there was a sudden cloud of red and then nothing and a stillness like it could never have been otherwise. Khan watched me the whole time and then he spoke. He says you must not understand. And then he had laughed.

He says you have made a mistake coming to him like this. That you showed your weakness too early. The interpreter put a nervous look at Khan and Khan nodded, his eyes bouncing and shining in a way that betrayed a quiet amusement. A cat pawing at a bird fallen out of its nest.

He says it is a shame because he would have liked, how do you say, the struggle? No, he would have liked to test himself against you, yes, *test himself*, if you had not made it so easy. He says you made it too easy for him and that he is disappointed. He says he thought you were a dangerous one to cross. But now he is not so sure.

Khan blackened. He fixed me across the table.

And he says you cannot frighten him.

I looked right back, showing nothing.

He says he is an old man and that he has seen many things. When the Russians came they burned away the crops and the animals and the earth. They put out the sun. Many Pashtun died. At night he and his men would stalk the Russian camps. They would steal soldiers away in the night and skin them while they were still alive and fix them on the hilltops.

Khan spoke in soft, emotionless tones, his lips barely moving.

Then the Russians would come into the villages. They would flame the houses. They would execute the mullah and the elders and tie the bodies to their tanks and drag them through the bazaar until there was nothing left at the ends of their ropes. Then they would molest the women. He says that for many months at a time the villages would give the Russians food and shelter and that the Russians would take their fighting away up into the hills. And he says that in other months they would go to live amongst the hills and they would murder the Russians while they slept and he says by day they would knock helicopters out of the sky and they would fight from the mountainside and live from the earth like their grandfathers before them. It is the Pashtun way. To survive. And there is great honour in survival.

Khan turned and spat against the white tiles.

He says he is an old man and he has seen many things and he is not so easy to frighten.

The interpreter wiped his shirtsleeve over his face.

I have no interest in frightening him. Tell him that.

He says that you speak of friendship and brotherhood, and that these are easy things to speak of. That they mean nothing. That such things as friendship and brotherhood and loyalty are the happy prizes of the poor or the stupid. That where life is very hard survival is everything. He says this is something you cannot know, that you cannot understand. That survival is maybe the greatest honour of all.

Khan sat back in his chair and pulled his cloak tight and up over his shoulder. He laid his hands palmdown against the table with the prayer beads threaded over-under the fingers on his left hand and his chin raised square off his chest.

He says if you have nothing else then it is time for him to leave.

I am not finished.

The interpreter kneaded his hands on his lap, looking first at me then across at Khan.

You are right, of course. To live. To live is the great honour.

Pause.

And why should I understand? I'm a foreigner. Rich. Spoiled. Godless. Too much comfort in life puts fat on the soul. It makes you greedy for everything and never satisfied so that things lose their meaning.

I took a slow drink of water, my hand showing steady on the glass.

But it's strange. You talk of survival and living at all costs and of brotherhood being a prize for the weak. But I'm not so sure. I'm not sure at all. It seems to me that where survival is above all else it is not a man's loyalties that speak of his waste and excesses, but his enemies. And your enemy is coming. Though he has yet to raise his rifle in anger he is as fated to you as the sunrise.

Pause.

We face the same enemy now, Khan. He won't negotiate with warlords and drug barons any more than he'll negotiate with heathen like me. The choice is simple. Do what must be done now. Or fight and die alone.

Somehow it made me think of that mangy old dog hunting for scraps and the way it had been there one moment and the brief flash of red and the echo of the gunshot coming back at us off-kilter like a snare drum snapping out of time and the nothingness that had followed.

After this Khan was very still and I watched the play come back into his eyes and he watched me and then he turned to the interpreter and then he sat back. He looked out into the yard. Finally he spoke. When he spoke it was like he was reminding himself of something he had almost forgotten.

He says, it is not the running around, but what is written on the forehead.

Afterwards he leaned back into his chair and he looked out into the yard over my shoulder and soon after he left.

I watched our marines readying for the offensive at dawn with the sky colouring over the outer walls and the dirt and rocks giving up the night cold so that there was a sharpness to the morning that was also a promise of the heat of the day to come. It was very near the end. Many flights home had been rescheduled to accommodate the offensive and there was a feeling that this was bad luck, although no one spoke openly of such things. That too was bad luck. The marines were quiet and there was none of that wonderful sickness that comes before battle that I had known before. I felt guilty that I was not with them, and relief, and much guilt.

The Afghan Kandak led the assault into Babaji. By midday the sound of heavy machine gun fire could be heard from across the river. When the reports began coming in we heard of many Afghan casualties along the northern flank and companies becoming pinned down along the high ground and the colonel walked the operations room calling orders to his staff officers with an affected and deliberate composure so that he was indistinguishable from the moment and afterwards it left a feeling of having watched an over-rehearsed scene with all the life and honesty gone out of it.

Then there was reporting that a convoy of armed vehicles had broken the enemy lines at Gholam Mohammad Kalay. The break tore open a movement corridor deep into Taliban-held territory in the east. There was talk of local militants leading a charge straight through the Kandak positions, the men leaning against the weight of their dushkas as their four-by-fours dropped blazing into the flood plain with the irrigated land and the gunnests below them. Marines supporting the charge counted dozens of enemy fighters gunned down along the road and lonely blood trails shrinking away into the ditches. By the time I heard that Haji Musa Khan had been killed at the head of the charge a breathless Afghan Brigadier had already slapped me on the shoulder and grinned at me through yellowed teeth and the smell of coffee on my face saying, you hear? you hear? they already calling him the Lion of Babaji, and we had watched the blinking mission screens and the blue positions lit up across the area of operations and we had sat there and there had been a feeling of the end and of many things not yet ended.

in the morning we are assembled without notice and the men file quietly into the gymnasium and form up in ranks to make an open square, myself and Lofty and several other troop officers stood easy to close off the hollow side, and there is an unease that is like herd animals before a storm, a commotion of swivelling eyes to repudiate a poise they affect out of long habit, their many straightbacked stillnesses; and the CO enters to a braced room, the RSM at his heel, only the click of boots across the sprungfloor and a wind that is come down off the hills to noise the parade ground, and in his theatre he eyeballs the front rank with intent in a way that intimates no single small detail will be overlooked or forgotten; short, deliberate steps, a medley of bronzed skins and fresh bright soft faces; and at the conclusion he raises his chin and says simply, gentlemen: give generously; the room braced once again to receive his departure; the RSM clicks his fingers and two corporals breach the double swingdoors heaving a large cardboard packing crate that scores and squeaks as they manoeuvre front and centre, the unmovement of men taking tiny nervous trots inside their boots: the crate about five feet by two and wrapped in layers of brown parcel tape in various stages of perishment and scrappy childish scrawls of black marker upon each face it tells: Mne Tait, P059331M; doodled genitilia spurting dramatically; and the RSM unhitches his beltknife and runs it over the top, marines craning their necks from the rearmost ranks, and he sinks his arm inside and rummages and he pulls out a thick patterned jacket that he hoists high for the men to see and he turns it over in his hand and smiles as though each view reveals some new and unforeseen connoisseurial delight: gents, do I have a fuckin treat in store for you today, this is an absolutely genuine pusser's thermal, one previous owner, stuffed with only the very finest pigeon feathers and guaranteed to take on water at the first hint of rain, only worn two or three hundred times previously with – sniffing at it, his eyebrows arching – jesus-me, with a much sought-after aroma of ballsack to round off this compelling proposition, very rare, only several hundred thousand ever made to my knowledge, what do I have? someone start me off; a low murmur of voices that runs through the ranks like a catching flame, a sudden thrill of curiosity and then amusement, and a voice from the back calls tenner; thank you, he says; fifteen sir calls another; I'll have it for thirty calls another; good, thank you; forty; I've got forty so far, will someone give me fifty? the RSM snarling the open flank in strides, a voice that he makes you feel down in your guts as if to rouse the massed ranks of timid souls to violence and glory on the eve of war; come on you tightfisted cunts he says, pay day tomorrow, I want to hear you shaking the moths out of your wallets, I want to see them pockets emptied if it means getting your oppo and shaking him down by the fuckin boots; and the jacket goes finally for eighty and the room is alight in something like uproar, and a single flip flop then goes for a hundred and two and three troop club together for an unused set of issue longjohns for three fifty and bonzo ends up donating an eyebrow for a round five hundred that he does there and then, sat on an upwise bucket with the RSM leaning over to nick it away in three triumphant strokes, and the crate is emptied only partially of shit and tat in those couple hours for a vast amount of money that will go to sweeten, in its modesty, the ashy mouthful of a loved one's desolation, and we are all of us throated and wild as men in a bloodlust, our brotherhood exceeds us, we are gratefully obliterated within it, and that night we go on into the streets like the victors of some sacked city and I drink beer and tequila at a bar until I can sour that feeling in my stomach, and it will be many years from now, looking back on it all with the kind of detached curiosity of a scholar consulting a text, before I see also that which is stood there faithfully at my shoulder, shadowed, indistinct, familiar, a single possessive hand rested upon me

After he left for the fighting, Patrick's mother began to advance the notion among us that two rather peculiar developments had occurred in relation to his father. These developments were thus: his apparent transformation into a man, shall we say, *newly troubled* by the strains of paternal devotion; and his conversion to the arcane delights of dry stone walling. It makes me chuckle to imagine it. Her, recounting these charges over a choppy satellite line beaming itself halfway around the other side of the world into desert and scrub. And Patrick thinking to himself, *nonsense*, or, she never really did *get* the old man, did she?

I can vouch for part of her claim. There's a story in there. The rest we'll have to hang on trust and best guesses.

Patrick's mother was from another time. That's how I'd describe her. A petite woman with modest appetites, modest vices. She drank a finger of amaretto with a halfglass of cranberry juice, twice, on a Friday evening. She kept her dinnertable clean of even tertiary greyshade profanity: jeez, frick, frig, feck, freak, fudge, fetch, beggar, shoot, dang, heck and hell. The whole shebang.

She had acted faithfully in the self-appointed role of guardian, purveyor and curator of the Gorman family history for about as long as I had known her. Some of the others liked to dismiss her testament as honest, oh yes, but *ultimately deluded*. Wishful thinking. And they would cock their heads and nod so with a delicious pitysmile on their faces, as though solemnly narrating a neighbour's crops lain waste by borers and rootworm. Superficially, I suppose, one is hard-pressed to disagree: there was what the women on the PTA termed a 'propaganda drive' a few years back after Patrick drove his father's Volvo through the shopfront window of the Post Office on the hard turn into the village; her insistence in the weeks to come that 'the incident' (it was only ever spoken of afterwards with quotation fingers and knowing eyes) was little more than high spiritedness gone awry, adolescent japery. A few of us heard the yelling before, the sieved sludge of hard voices through soft walls. We knew. But she had actually used the word japery. I liked her for that.

Calling her deluded though. That was just wrong-headed through and through. I knew her well enough to say she had an uncommon eye for observation when she wanted, for getting deep under things. An eye for detail to stop you dead in your shoes and make you feel like she has a tongue-wetted finger paging through the open ledgerbook of your most secret life. The simple sum of things was that she saw it all, I mean really saw things cold and plain, but that she refused to apportion blame or keep a running tally on guilt and its accumulated interest. The womenfolk in the town viewed this as a tragedy and a weakness; the same, I imagine, as if she had been struck under by some wasting disease. And they disgorged their scorn on Patrick and his father many times over in recompense for her lack as the sole cause of that family's, that poor *woman's* troubles. But for me that refusal to blame, those manifold and earnest explanations for the misfortunes that life had visited her, expressed some kind of deeply realised understanding of how scraps and debris and chance all play their part shaping the courses of our own crooked little paths. The impossibility of saying *I know this person and I know why they do the things they do*. I like to think that, in its own way, her cosy constancy of belief was evidence of a clear-sighted and revolutionary spirit. Although this is one instance where we'll have to go with a little bit of trust. A little bit of best guessing.

And so her toughest break, that which would eventually become her raison d'être, was the charge to justify the thing that existed between Patrick and his father. The coolness that had crept up between them that had once been a brief and sumptuous and easy love (I had seen it for myself), what had turned to mutual awe, incomprehension perhaps, whilst Patrick was still an infant, then slowly to silence and to the hardening of that incomprehension into suspicion and muted hostility, and then, at the end, to a tough blue frost. Frost and ambivalence. The coolness that had crept up unnoticed and pleasant like a summer breeze that had gone to glue deep in their arteries and finally bore them apart from each other. Two dogs tearing each other to rags over a big old bone with more than enough meat on it for the both of them. Too much the same, too much the same, and therein the tragedy. To this problem and this alone she attributed solely the unknowable solitudes and mysteries of Men.

And what of his father? I'm no man to judge heart or soul but I knew him well enough to bear witness to his earthly habits. Looking back I would say we had probably been friends long enough for us to forget what it was we had first valued between us but not yet long enough for us to entirely unlearn the habit of companionship. I'd hazard that such arrangements are more commonplace than many of us would care to admit. It'll suffice for an excuse in any case.

He was foreman at the factory where I had worked before Patrick was born. A drunk and a charmer and a man whose passions had gently, opiately, degraded to time-killing. I think this lot suited him about right. No longer able to exploit the romanticism that made the hard drinking and the gambling of his youth like something godly, something courageous, he was still able to summon a kind of magic for his dead hobbies that could really turn a conversation, could somehow grab a moment and fix it right there, right in front of you, fully-formed and ripe and appetising. He could still polish up a drinking story to a decent glassball shine. And as far as I knew he had never had any truck with building walls, dry stone or otherwise, nor with any manual labour or exertion beyond the factory floor that didn't conclude directly with a cold beer and a pout and a stagefront position at the bar.

She told me once about how he liked to waltz when he had whisky in his belly. How his hands would go soft like a boy's and his eyes would lose that frantic, windswept quality, and how they would dance in the privacy of their living room to the smoke and the sad of This Nearly Was Mine. How that was like a glimpse through a lifetime haze of frustration and little cruelties into a forgotten place of sweetness. Of deep regret.

There was that thing with Patrick, but only until he went away. After that everything changed. Or so I heard.

The first of it came to me through old man Delaney. Delaney had been there at the factory since even I was a lad and he knew its peculiar dynamic, that blissful deepbore catatonia of career clockwatching, intimately enough to have a kind of animal sensitivity to any atmospheric disturbance that needled infinitesimally off the norm. Arthritis had his limbs fixed and jagged like a figurine. He was all angles. That was how he drank his beer while we were sitting there: all angles and sharp movement and him tipping his head to the glass.

He told me that Patrick's father had recently taken to working up conversation over the breaktime kettle. It didn't seem to matter all that much who he was speaking to and the conversation didn't require much in the way of a response. He just wanted to talk. And he would talk about his boy, and *did you know* (Delaney shaking his index finger at me the same way that Patrick's father would spike his sentences), *did you know* that Patrick is part of 148 Battery? which is basically a part of the Special Boat Service, even though they don't wear the same cap badge, but it's close enough to count, and, just think of it! my boy in the Special Forces, *well*, he always had been an outdoorsy lad, I should have known it from the time he swam the Firth of Forth on New Year's day that year for a dare, do you remember me telling you? all that way in the freezing cold, I had half a mind to box seven shades of brown out of him when he got home, but oh, oh I should have realised then. These soldiers, the really good ones, they have a *type* you know, not many people can do the sort of work they do. And this 148 Battery is an elite outfit, really it is, working alongside those Special Forces and calling in artillery strikes behind enemy lines, and Patrick doesn't say it to us because I know he doesn't want his mother worrying, but I'm pretty sure he's been deep behind the lines already, probably causing all sorts of trouble knowing him, and it's only a shame his granddad isn't alive to see him now, he'd be a proud man, a very proud man indeed – And old man Delaney catching the astonishment working across my face and saying:

Honest to God. Honest to God. I've never heard him talk so much in all the time I've known him. And that's all well and good but it's getting to the point where no one wants to be the first man to get the coffee on the go at the risk of getting caught up in it. Ten minutes for a break isn't long enough at the best of times.

And what do you think it is? Is it a pride thing? Is he just enjoying his time in the limelight?

Pause.

I don't think it's that. – His eyes rolling around in their sockets a little with that soft, punch-drunk look he had going – He says it all with a smile on his face, so you might think it was bragging if you didn't know any better. But there's something else too. Like you can imagine him suddenly grabbing you by the collar and getting all close in your face and just begging you for something.

Begging? Begging for what?

I don't know. But begging. That's the feeling I get underneath it; like he's begging you for something he can't ask for and you can't give. And I can't say it's something I like all that much either. Now, are you going to buy me another beer or are you just gonna sit there and watch an old man near as damnation die from thirst?

I went out to see him where he was working on the wall. It was about two feet high by then, skirting the front of the old barn from the stable end and tracking along a guiding wire that ran parallel to the threshing floor. The stones were clean and smooth and wet from the morning fog. He came through the clearing over the road with a plastic sack over his shoulder and when he saw me he showed neither surprise nor interest. His cheeks were red and wet and his exhaustion seemed like a happiness of itself.

Wall's coming along then.

Yes.

Much left to do?

Some. – Pause – Need to get these top courses laid before the winter cold comes in. Disrupts the setting otherwise.

Of course.

The end's good and firm though. – Pointing over to where the stone was packed in under a wooden A-frame – That's the worst of it beat.

Slow work.

Nodding. Slow work.

Pause.

You'll have to bring me out when it's finished.

Yes.

Patrick's mother had said he would be like this. Said he had been trolling the quarry for weeks now to find the right field stones for the wall and had hauled them across one sack at a time. We were blowing our coffees and she was talking at me all nimble and fleet: *At the weekend* he comes in after dark, exhausted, sometimes as late as seven or eight, and filthy. Absolutely filthy. Sort of happy and dirty and kind. And he scrubs himself up and I make him a hot scotch toddy and he sits himself down and he reads for the evening (actually reads, can you believe it) and afterwards he'll tell me about the things he has read, about those stone walls that date right the way back to the Bronze Age and how they are like vandalism against the gods or somesuch, and I try to understand but really, it's like a foreign language to me, but I try to keep up, I do, and when he's had a good day at it he sleeps like a little boy, just like Patrick when he was a child. And oh, it is *wonderful* to see him this interested in something.

That's what she told me. Of course, I'd already heard talk of the wall-building from Mrs Fowler, that conduit of local happenstance and gossip, and there had been mention too at the book club that Patrick's father had been considering renovating the barn. Something along those lines. But all of it sounded strangely incongruent, somehow off-key, at least until I heard her say it for herself.

I remember us talking lightly of other things and then the conversation lazing back onto itself, and after only a minute or two *he* had righted himself stubbornly between us as the subject and the centre of our conversation. She edged towards me in a conspiratorial lean though there was only the two of us and she told me how she had caught him watching rolling news coverage – those were her words – and I stopped her and I said, caught him?

how do you mean, *caught him*? and she told me how she had recently started walking in on him watching the news when he couldn't sleep at night or when she arrived home early from school, and she described how it had become somehow seedy and unwholesome (not for me, oh no, but for him, just in the way he looks at me when I catch him: embarrassed, angry: and in its own way that makes it shameful for me as well, do you see?). She told me that he didn't take any more of a role than he used to in writing letters or emails to Patrick, nor in speaking to him on the phone on those rare, hurried calls. Nothing except the usual blunted and rhetorical pleasantries. But that he would creep by the phone. That's another of the words she used, *creep*, as though describing something base and primal about the very mechanism of the act itself; a guilt or a lust, like a household pet drawn terribly and thrillingly and inescapably towards kitchen smells. She told me how the evening before he had stood out in the front garden and watched the traffic for almost an hour. Just standing there, watching. I could feel all of this leading somewhere and I said, but look, I don't get it. I really don't get it. Rolling news? Letters and emails and phone calls? I shrugged, dumb, and she opened her hands and laughed as though explaining something wonderfully elementary that only needed a kind and patient voice to invoke its revelation. And she said, oh don't you see, don't you see? It's *him* he's waiting for.

And so I had come to see the wall with my own eyes. Like it might give design and surface to everything else that was happening back then. I couldn't know about him suddenly becoming a strange and doting father. How could anyone? But I found out about the wall alright. That's the part of all this I can tell you near enough true and proper, far as it pays to put any faith in what I have to say.

Anyway. Love and compulsion. It's all part of the same sickness, isn't it?

*

Patrick came home. In the town they said he had seen some of the fighting.

At dinner that night we toasted to homecomings and good health and to absent friends. Patrick behaved impeccably. He sat very straight in his chair. He had never been a tall boy but he carried himself now so that he seemed to fill a space two or three times over. Duncan Hennessey buried his curiosity with a workmanlike rendering of uninterest and Juliette Hennessey buried her lack of interest with a workmanlike rendering of curiosity so that, between them, they managed an agreeably diplomatic conversational line. Only the slightest of jarring notes to an ear attuned to such things. Patrick nodded courteously throughout and expressed himself in tidy, authoritative sentences, lean of any unnecessary weight. A smile garnished as an afterthought. He insisted on pouring the drinks: sparkling wine and then a chilled white Burgundy for the starter and a heavyweight Argentinian red to follow with the lamb.

His father drank quickly that night and said little. It was difficult to read him. I was coming at him with coloured eyes and I couldn't shake off the stories I'd heard. At a push I would say the only thing he did was look at that boy with a quiet awe. There's that phrase, *hanging on every word*. That's what it was like: Patrick spoke and his father seemed to attend the things he said with keenness and great concentration, as if sifting those words for hidden meaning, unheralded depths, and his chin would lift and drop as though buoyed by an invisible thread to the lilting patterns of his voice.

The conversation danced and potted and only occasionally glanced up against the edges of that which we could not speak of directly. The Hennesseys' skiing holiday in Kitzbuhel and the price of petrol and press intrusion and freedom of the press and the best way to roast lamb and the merits and pitfalls of barbequing and piracy off the Horn of Africa and the price of petrol. Finally, inexorably, we came to the wall. There was an off-joke to start and laughter across the table and Patrick's mother boiling a look of mock disapproval. Duncan Hennessey: Moving swiftly on then. Now do tell us. Julie and I are dying to know. What *have* you been doing with that old barn? Patrick's father parried their questions, bashful and flustered and unsteady, and then the boy joined them and his brittle defences seemed to crumble to nothing right in front of us:

Oh well now. It's nothing much really. Just a hobby. I've been wanting to rebuild the stone wall that used to sit along outside the barn, is all. I remembered it from when I was only a boy myself, although it was half broken down even then. Till all the grass and the moss grew in it and lifted it apart and then it was just rubble for a while and after that the rubble went off with the wind and rain and under the ground and there was nothing left.

He's done such a wonderful job.

That's all there is. It keeps me busy. Keeps my hands busy.

And lost such a lot of weight too. Doesn't he look good for it?

I'll take you along to see it tomorrow. If you like. It's almost done.

I agreed, of course. We set a time to meet. But it wasn't me he was asking. Patrick agreed too. It set the unhurried quality of a smile deep in his father's eyes. Like the sudden still and weightlessness of a field over which the wind has just died.

Talk got to politics as we got drunker. Patrick's mother riding a blank hostess smile, Juliette Hennessey sunk into visible boredom. We became ashamed or afraid to talk of the fighting, I can't remember which. Like just saying the word might raise up the recently dead among us in that dining room. And because we were ashamed or afraid or both but still mad in our curiosity we spoke of it in blowy and abstract terms.

I was talking. Slightly drunk and knowing:

Well we had a bash two times before and the Russians had a crack at it too and no one has yet managed to win a war against the Afghans. That's the truth of it. Is this time different? Is it? – Swilling the bowl of my glass – You know what? I think maybe it is. From what I've read, I mean. (To Patrick: I don't pretend to be an expert, so do correct me if I'm wrong). The politicians seem genuinely committed to tying up the war effort to a political solution. That's a good start, isn't it? And all this talk of negotiations with the Taliban. I think that's a fundamental step to be taken. It's distasteful, certainly. But if we learned anything from the Troubles, then surely it was the necessity for compromise and dialogue.

The problem is you're coming at it from an exit-strategy perspective, said Duncan Hennessey, also slightly drunk and knowing. When in fact, we haven't even yet defined the reasons for going to war in the first place. Do excuse me, Patrick. It goes without saying that what you and your colleagues you have done is beyond comprehension for any of us here, something for which we as a country are honestly and wholeheartedly grateful. – Pause – But the fact remains that without clear reasons for *why* we went to war in the first place, all those so-called solutions and negotiations are little more than escape routes disguised by politicians without the balls for the fight. It's simple economics. If you'll forgive me for saying as much, Patrick. War and conflict generates big business. Politicians like the military because it galvanises public opinion in their favour and it fills their coffers and it gives them a grandstand on the world stage. But long war drains the coffers and it drains public opinion and it turns that opiate of the masses into a clunking albatross of a foreign policy decision. *That* is why you need sound reasons for going to war: because one day you will need sound reasons for leaving. And that – he concluded, cracking his knuckles on one hand as though surprised by his steady eloquence, his fortuitous arrival at a place of passable interest – is why mission creep is *the* unforgivable sin of military strategy in the twenty-first century.

Oh, I don't know about any of that.

It was the first I remembered Patrick's father volunteering anything all night. The table went suddenly quiet for the novelty.

All this talk about money and politics. If you ask me, the real question is how can we *not* be in that country? Eh?

He seemed pleased with this and let it settle for effect.

You want to hand it back to those vicious medieval thugs? They're half crazy for starters. Did you know they banned VCRs and music and nail polish? Even clapping, for God's sake. And I was reading about how they cut off the women's noses. How they'd throw acid in their faces or bury them alive or beat them in the streets. Just the thought of it makes me sick in my stomach. How can we not have a moral duty to protect those people? Can someone explain that to me?

Pause. His cheeks were shining.

Ask Pat. He'll tell you, won't you lad?

Pause.

Patrick. What do you say on the matter?

Oh I don't know, dad.

Come on. You know what it's really like out there.

Oh I don't know. It's not for me to say. I'm just a soldier. Leave the politics to the politicians, that's what I reckon. Seems to work ok.

But you've got to have a view on things. How can you not have a view on things?

Pause.

It's just…I don't know. – Shrugging his palms in defeat – I guess I still haven't got to understanding how one life can ever be worth sacrificing. For a cause. For anything. It's something I just can't get my head around.

There was a long, dead silence. Duncan Hennessey leant back and folded his hands on his lap and set the frame of his chair acreak. The magnanimous blank of his face bellowed a victory.

Let me clear the plates.

I'll help, Patrick said.

I watched Patrick's father swallow hard and I watched him look down at his plate with an expression that was boyish in the wholeness and the sincerity of its not understanding, and he sniffed once, casually, and took a quick drink from his glass and set his jaw and I thought of him standing out there watching the traffic pass with an autumn sun oxidising bronze and rust and gunmetal and rosewater above the houses and I thought of him knelt down at the side of the wall black to the knees and his hands ribboned with calluses. And I had that feeling from when I was a child when I thought of my parents and the things they had done for me: a rich, hopeless love mixed up in a swill of guilt and sadness and a sense that I had somehow neglected a charge of protection over them once entrusted to me.

After coffee Patrick opened the port and we drank until the decanter was emptied.

The Hennesseys left. We were very drunk but we had eaten enough so that the drink made us sluggish and malleable and didn't turn us nasty. Patrick's father left to pick up a six-pack from a late night store and we made a gentle mockery of him in his absence and Patrick's mother scolded us with a smile and sipped at peppermint tea and we talked about the future and of bright things and of sleep. An hour later, when his father still hadn't returned, his mother drove us first to the off-licence, and then to the supermarket and the petrol station and then back through the high street. Patrick was silent and kept shaking his head. The roads were empty at that time and a storm was working itself out slick and cold on the roads. The wipers turned the windscreen to streetlight colours. By the time we made it home the drink had gone out of us from worry and frustration. We found him sitting in the porch with an open case of beer between his legs and his boots black to the ankle with mud and rainwater.

Forgot my keys, he said.

*

It was midday. The air was wet and breathy and it still had the taste of the rain on it and the three of us stood in a row like mourners at a graveside. The far end of the wall was spilled out on the ground, the A-frame snapped and the pieces scattered over the rubble. I was standing there rooted to myself and Patrick had his hands in his hair saying, Jesus, dad, what happened? and he bent down amongst the stones with his hands hovering outstretched in clairvoyant mediation, uncertainly, inexpertly, as though hoping to compel the waste to sculpt itself back into order and shape, and he ended up just squatted there into his ankles and running his hands through his hair saying, Jesus, dad, what happened? What do we do? And we looked over to his father where he was stood off to one side, staring down at the wall, detached and ferocious in a way that made me think of a general appreciating the spread of his forces across a tabletop, and he stuffed his hands into his pockets and shrugged his shoulders and turned off towards the car.

When I told his mother about the wall she stopped and looked past me. As though remembering something.

Oh, she said. How terrible. She leaned against the counter.

Probably those storms.

Pause.

Yes, she said. Probably.

Outside the first lights along the street were just coming on. The twilight was still back behind the rooftops, pooling silent amongst the flower beds and alleyways like something hesitant.

saturday morning and the grey of the city and I am running errands, I am late to collect my daughter, and the streets are thick with people smalled against a cold march wind, they walk with their heads buried in their shoulders and their arms stiff with shopping and they are grave and preoccupied in their efforts and I do not know yet that I am sick, and it is unshaped in your mind and on your lips but in your secret heart you cannot understand how this world did not halt in its turn when you left it, that the old women would persist in the kindly discipline of their habits, jute shopping bags unfolded conscientiously from tartan canvas trolleys, their slow precise palmfuls of coins, that the children by the statue can play and squabble and be innocent yet of the ravages their fathers have conceived, that the day is white and flat and unremarkable and as it is now so it has been before and so it will be again, and perhaps this is what it is like to be dead; and I collect my change from the cashier and she is already hurried to the next before I can thank her and my movements are ponderous, dulled with emphasis, my limbs feel oversized and a little ridiculous, and they scutter around me like insects and I step among them as though shining in a cold light, outside of their many smallnesses, the modesty of their experiences, and I am impossibly strong and I am without feature because that which cannot be reckoned in relativity cannot be reckoned at all, and I do not look into the windowglass as I leave for fear I will not find myself in it; and from the party my daughter skips across the pavement cracks and chatters to herself and she seems to play a chattery cheerful practical woman deep in her imaginings, her hand like a teaspoon in mine, and on the bus there are the earliest signs of it though I don't know them yet as signs, some alignment of the engine noise and the press of wind-smelling bodies and the running condensation on the windows that achieves it, that makes my lungs dry and my fingernails to find the underside of my seat and I am kind of shrinking into myself and she says daddy, daddy, tugging at my sleeve and I smile and I behave my breathing and this seems just enough to convince her and she exchanges her concern for a question, something about why did the pink bear try to kill the cowboy that I answer, deadpan and ad-libbed, to her visible confusion; and I am at my mother's door watching them rub noses, something I have not seen before, it reminds me that seven months for a man is but one ascent across an endless vista of rugged country when for a child it is a precipice without foot or summit, and she pours me tea into familiarly chipped china and she says I should be getting more sleep and she tells me about my brother and his family and she tells me about the church hall that is being torn down for flats and my daughter races the coffee table, butterfly and helicopter, and I am staggered with wonder and with horror that the very least of these, the smallest particularity should have been spared when many mighty unassailable unspeakable things have been swept away and given up to the depths and lost even from the faithful remembrance of the earth

Using procedures to separate the physical and emotional traumas, the scientists trained the rats using "fear conditioning" techniques two days after they experienced a concussive brain trauma... "Something about the brain injury rendered them more susceptible to acquiring an inappropriately strong fear. It was as if the injury primed the brain for learning to be afraid."

– Fanselow et al

*

It was at sixteen hundred feet when my primary chute failed, and it was somewhere near eleven hundred when the reserve chute tangled and collapsed in on itself, popping like a gunshot. I couldn't tell you where it was I passed out. They said that was lucky, the passing out, that my body gone soft and floppy in free fall must have sucked up some of the impact. Someone said I bounced, and that that was a good sign. I came away from it with a pelvic fracture, a femoral shaft fracture, five cracked ribs, a punctured lung, internal bleeding, multiple facial fractures, and trauma to my neck, spine and brain. A full house. At the hospital they stuck me full of morphine and titanium and well-wishers made cracks about me never getting through airport security again. It had been my fifth jump.

After they got me stable I was moved to the neurological ward of the defence rehabilitation centre at Headley Court. They put my legs and face in metal cages to set the bone right, with fat metal rods sticking out of my skin in severe-looking spoking patterns. My legs pliable and weltered and cookiedough soft under the sheets. They wired me up to an overhead pulley system and they fixed my neck in a collar to protect my face from the weight of my own head. Trussed up like that I could see only this narrow band of ceiling on the opposite side of the ward, even with my eyes doing a full roll in their sockets. I can still picture it now: wall and ceiling laced faintly with cobwebs and cracking varnish; a scroll of ornamental plasterwork trim running split through the middle. Some shitty creamcoloured pillbox aperature onto the world alright. They had me bedded close by the swingdoor entrance to the ward and the through traffic announced itself with the sweep and bang of the doors, a flush of floor polish on cold corridor air, with these voices that stirred and blinked around me. It was a kind of blindness, having my face set away from the world like that, and it got so I could soon tell the time by the windowed sunpatterns that rose and stretched and dialled and shrank across my line of sight, could place a nearby patient by the character of their footfall or, at a distance, by words scattered soft and indiscriminate and indistinct.

At the time the neuro ward was housed in the east wing of the old rehabilitation complex that had been converted after the war and then abandoned to steady ruin. It had the potted staleness of a museum or garden shed. The smell of damp carpet came on with the morning and it went cool and green and lush and mildewey with the afternoon light. I had this feeling of stickiness on my face and fingers the whole time. A Sister Nikita worked the floor five days a week. She talked to herself as she attended her chores, asking what it was to work in these conditions, asking, ach, heavens, is this how we are to be treated? her voice glottal and fatted like she was speaking through twin dumplings trapped in her gullet. I never caught her straight on but the sister was a big press of fless with garlic always on her breath, a familiar presence about the edges of my vision, and she was rough and kind, and in the way she went about things you could figure she had come to the job full of fire, and that she'd been beaten down by a ton of slight disappointments and slight horrors over a ton of slight and sorry years, and her kindness now was sort of mechanical and hollow and fully realised in its own act, like the frantic, heartfelt action of a swing long after the kid has bailed from his seat. But that was ok. Kindness out of habit or obligation has still a little heft to it, still counts for something. That was something I came to appreciate in those first days.

What with my face fixed up I couldn't see the other patients, but I got to know them by their screams. They were mostly soldiers that had become brain damaged during the fighting. All of them carried injuries and some were double or triple amputees. Their days started early and ran to a military schedule and in the mornings the nurses took them out to shit, shower n shave in time for first parade. They were usually pretty upbeat and cheerful milling about in their fresh uniforms, in their hot red polished skins, and listening to them with only my drabness of ceiling in consort got me thinking of my own happy barrackroom memories: hotly macho, modest, playful – hey, new guy, want me to grab you a Coke or something for when we get back? me, I'm gonna smash fifteen pull-ups today, nothing to it, you heard it here first, gonna show that Colours Senior who the real fucking cripple is, hey catch you later, don't go anywhere now while we're out, ok? (laughter) – their footsteps a mixed scatter of soft-soled shoes and prosthetics and rubbertoed crutches tapped out into the long, echoing corridors. By day many of them were still fighting the wars they had come home from.

By night they entertained horrors and unspeakable slicks of guilt and Sister Nikita ran her rounds, soothing them at their fevered bedsides, never forgetting to visit me last though I, usually spatchcocked off the last painkiller roller, hardly ever made a whimper.

There was the guy I named Foghorn. Foghorn shit us all up equally. Out of the night stillness, out of nothing, he would bolt suddenly upright in his bed and scream his guts up into the darkness, till his voice ground out all hoary and dry and shredded, until whatever it was pitchforking his dreams either had its fill or got bored enough to let him slink away into meagre halfsleep. It was a fucker not to be able to turn my head away from it, from this rippy piercing quality that caught my left eardrum sweetly every time and made the stuff inside my bones shiver. Things like that stay with you. Then there was Shits. Shits would ruin his bedclothes when the nightmares came. Those midnight smells were the worst, with the beds being stripped of their sheets and this chewy iron tannin of undressed wounds you could taste on the flats of your tongue. Those smells could find me out in the deep, eerie underworld places the drugs sometimes took me, places where even the screams didn't fully carry. And then there was Sinatra, who normally picked up just before dawn, starting off in a low soft puppy moan for his *mummy mummy oh mummy* that would pitch to wailing and high shrieks and would end with him bleating wetly into the bedsheets. Sinatra had shot his best friend in the face in a contact (everyone on the ward knew it) and the sister would sit with him and tell him over and over that it was only an accident, that it wasn't his fault. Strapped up in my caging, hearing that shit repeated at a distance in my funky yellow halfsleep, I got to thinking maybe she might have been talking to me, wondering what accident it was that I'd committed and how I might ever be forgiven for it. That was how it was. The nights were warm and long and sorry and soursmelling and it was some small mercy that the daylight always made it somehow softed and difficult to remember, garbled in its transmission like a message carried off man-to-man down a line.

And then there was the guy in the bed opposite. Just like me, I never once heard him make a noise in the night. But there was something about the way he held his quiet that caught my attention. A kind of livewire quietness you'd normally put down to concentration, to purposed amounts of intense, silent activity. He never snored or sounded out deep sleeping breaths, but I'd wake into the darkly morning hours and I could feel that quietness as something substantial and animate and darker still against the pallor of another unbroken dawn. I got this feeling he was watching or waiting on something. Observing the night wildnesses of the ward. We got to talking on one of those first mornings. His was a voice like a mastiff barking at garden shadows.

Hey. Hey you, bandages.

Me?

Yeah you, who else?

Sorry. I can't see a fucking thing with this neck brace on.

Figures. Well it's just the two of us in here. Just you and me.

How come you're not out there in rehab with the rest of them?

I'm still getting operated on right now. They want me bedridden while they wait for the surgery to settle down and that before they move me about again. It's doing my nut in, stuck here with fuck all to do.

What happened?

I got blown up. Nothing glamorous, I just got unlucky. Stepped on an anti-tank mine with about half an inch of the tread of my boot. They reckon my mate Sonny had trod clean over the bastard before I set it off.

Did it get you bad?

You really can't see for shit, can you?

I can see the ceiling pretty well.

Huh. – Pause – Yeah well, it caused a bit of mischief like. I'm a bilat.

A bilat?

Bilateral transfemoral amputee. Two amputations above the knee.

Shit. I'm sorry.

And I've got a hole in the back of my head the size of half a cricket ball, which is why they've thrown me in with the rest of the nutjobs in this batshit crazy ward. They've got to check me for brain injury before I can rejoin the others. Hey, what about you?

You mean, what happened?

Yeah.

I fell out of a plane.

Pause.

Well why in the fuck did you do *that*?

Kyle, he said. 25200398 Corporal Kyle Franklin Summers, pleasure to fucking meet you. Kyle had been a talented water polo player before the attack and had considered leaving the Army to go full pro. He talked about that a lot. There were many other things we did not talk about.

His fiancé visited him every weekend, and for hours at a time in the afternoons there would only be the three of us in the ward, with me often forgotten entire to my silences and my wallwatching and my sultry squirmy bouts under the painkillers. I got to know when she was there before she said a word, sometimes before she was even in the room: her perfume went ahead of her and there was a kind of lightening of the room when she was around that was like an insistence of breeze or a dappled throw of sunlight. Summery and clean and welcome. She had a voice that any man with blood in him would have gone crazy over, and on the bones of it my imagination hung any number of Playboy-vanilla fantasies. A short and blowy summer dress. Watercolour curves. Wild tumble-blonde hair. She would read Kyle shit and curios from the papers, and she would update him on family trivia and how the wedding planning was progressing, and she would tell him over and over how well he looked and how quickly his strength seemed to be coming back and how soon he would be walking again, soon enough to walk her down the aisle, no doubt of it, and the sum effect of all this was always to drive Kyle further into himself, to make him sullen and unresponsive and spiky. I mean, he was a hard one to figure.

On Thursdays and Fridays, while the others were out on their rounds, Kyle would talk at me about her arrival that coming weekend and he would have this kid excitement to him that you could tell from the high thrill in his voice and from how he would muddle himself saying the same shit over and over and it not really mattering a whole lot whether I was there to listen or not – You've got to see her, when they've fixed you up proper mate. She's got a fine little arse on her and these legs, man, these legs that go on forever. And she's a good girl too, you know what I mean? She's been super cool about everything that's happened and all, I mean, she was in a shit state when I first got back and everything, of course you've gotta expect that, but better this than me coming home in a box right? but you know she's been there for me, really been there, I don't know what I'd do without her, and she's a class piece of skirt alright, you've got to see her, legs right up to the sky – But it was always the same: by mid-morning on Saturday he would have gone off into himself again and she would be coaxing measly crumbs of conversation out of him, grunts, shoulderslumps, and after she left he would be deeply blackly fixed and he would *not want to fucking talk, ok*? and I would lie there and I would watch my stripe of ceiling and I would leave my brain to scoot around down down in the tanglethickets of my delirium.

A few weeks in they started dialling down my medication. That helped me pull my head together. But it made the nights worse too: easier to rationalise, sure, but there were no more easy exits on a quick dope hit. With my head clearing I started noticing the way the others were around me. Foghorn and Shits and Sinatra and Marty and Rio and the others had a funny act going, kind of cautious and sympathetic and distanced, nothing at all like the feint and jab of their own talk. It was something similar with Kyle. After that first conversation he never asked me anything else about the accident, and this omission charged somehow with an air of self-satisfied restraint, genial tact perhaps of the highest order. It was as though, despite the variety of choice butchery on show, my wounds caused them a unique embarrassment. It took me a while to figure, not least because I was crashing hard on a fentanyl comedown. But it was simple enough: I had not fought and I had not been to the war and my wounds had not been forged by brass or explosives or hot slugs of liquid lead.

I told some of this to the brain doc, a neuro occupational therapist, and he said that was likely just paranoia. That paranoia was to be expected as a result of the extent of the concussion I had experienced. Because Kyle and I were still unable to leave our beds the therapist came to visit us when the ward was otherwise emptied during the main morning physio sessions, and he would close off the curtains as though that were sufficient to ensure patient confidentiality. He was this young ambitious guy full of bounce and readymeal sentences. He told me he was writing a paper on traumatic brain injury (he called it TBI on rote, kind of like how my mum took to dropping *Tony* into casual conversation after meeting the former PM at a book signing) that he hoped to have published in the New Year. Post traumatic stress was the poster child for veterans' home-side injuries at the time, and I suppose he felt like he was cutting some revolutionary furrow with the brain injury stuff, with his crop of fine, fresh, legless specimens. I picked him as a cold fucker, though I don't think he'd have believed that if I'd told it him to his face: the kind to confuse the passion they have for their work with the compassion they have for humanity, for the people around them. He asked me about my memories from the fall and about my short-term memory and about my mood, whether I was experiencing anxiety or depression or confusion, and all this other headshrink shit, and I always answered positively, truthfully, and the therapist seemed to finish our sessions disappointed and distracted. He had a voice on him like a nine iron hitting a high sweet short.

Kyle was good though. Kyle made it a sport. He could tie up a whole half-hour session talking around how, if he touched his temple with his index finger it would make his tongue taste copper. Or how he got really angry whenever anybody used the word *door*. Or how it gave him a hardon for anyone to run their finger around the inside of the crater at the base of his skull. The therapist lapped this shit up and he would go through pencils at a time saying, good, good, good, in his soothing clipped nine iron tones. Kyle was good fun when he wasn't in one of his black fixes and he was at his very best when he was running rings around this guy.

So let me get this straight in my head, doc. You don't mind if I call you doc, do you?

Not at all.

Thanks doc. So it's like this: so you're telling me that brain injuries sustained in a blast can actually be the *cause* of a guy beating his wife ten years down the line?

That's not quite it. Close though. See, traditional thinking has it that trauma can be sort of chopped into two, that you can break it down neatly into physical and psychological causes and physical and psychological outcomes. There's some token overlap, so I'm simplifying a little here. What I'm exploring with TBI is the extent to which psychological damage is exclusively rooted in the physical transformation of the brain. I mean, technically speaking, everything we experience is underpinned by physical change. That much is fact. But the orthodoxy still seems to hold that causation for things like PTSD and acute stress disorder exists entirely outside of actual literal physical adjustments to the brain itself, in some abstract unquantifiable realm of the emotions. And that they are therefore entirely treatable by non-physical treatment. Counselling and psycho-theraphy. That sort of thing.

Gotcha. Lots of cuddles, right doc?

Right. So what I'm looking at (and there's a wealth of new data coming out of Afghanistan on this stuff) is the way in which TBI appears to act as a primer for all the flashbacks and the depression and the reexperiencing phenomenom, and all that other messy stuff we used to lazily lump together as shell shock. In short, I think we can trace a clear link between brain injury sustained in battle and a psychological tendency to violence months or years down the line.

Holy shit, doc. So what you're telling me is that having a quarter of my skull blown out might actually be responsible for making me punchy in five or ten years?

Like I say, it's not quite so simple. But my theory would predict that two troops, experiencing a similar intensity of fighting and similar casualties over a similar period of time but differentiated by either their exposure to gun battles (like we saw a few years ago) or to IEDs (like the way things are now), where the brain gets rattled around a lot, would see highly variable long-term psychological outcomes. I would expect to see a far higher rate of suicide and domestic abuse, for example, in the latter sample. –

166

That was how he said it, ha, fucking *sample* – What I'm trying to push for now is better awareness, so that traditional post-trauma care is complemented by medical treatment to combat the effects of TBI. That's why I'm here really.

But if everything that happens has a physical cause –

A precedent. I prefer precedent.

If everything that happens to me has a precedent in the brain, then everything's fixed, right? Then shit's going to happen and there's nothing I can do to fix it. It's the ultimate get-out-of-jail-free card.

Transformation in the brain sets the *conditions* for decision-making. But I've yet to see it significantly alter a patient's ability to make free and informed decisions. TBI is an impairment like anything else. I mean, you'll be able to walk again soon enough, won't you? Maybe not in the way you've known it before, but walking nonetheless. We just have to learn to be creative in our fixing.

Holy shit, doc. You're blowing my mind with this stuff. If you'll excuse the pun.

It's an exciting line of work, I have to admit. And it's you guys that are right on the bleeding edge of it. – Pause – If you'll excuse the pun.

Hey, doc. You ever had a TBI?

No.

You ever been involved in a traumatic incident?

No, I can't say I have.

Huh.

The therapist tidied his papers and thanked Kyle for his time and he left. He was in a fine mood. You could hear it in his shoestep. There was this moment of silence in the room when there was briefly only the sound of the mower somewhere out on the grounds and then we went off into great rips of laughter, going at it so hard I could feel my broken chest banging against the cast.

Wow. What a tremendous bellend.

After Kyle had his stumpies fitted things were different, if only for a short while. They were very painful at first and his legs would bleed through in the evenings. But he was making quick progress and I soon became familiar with the sound of his stumpies pocking and sucking in careful, deliberate lines about his bedside. He was proud of the pain he suffered and he spoke of it the way a boxer might speak lovingly of the very best blows he has taken from a champion fighter. Kyle wasn't yet ready to move out of the neuro ward and Sister Nikita spent long hours with him by his bed and on the training bars, willing him forward from one leg to the next, ach, and never taking any shit from him when he humped and growled and spat. It was a good thing to hear. My head was cleaning up fast and I too was switching to thoughts of mending.

What made it hardest was the exceptionality of our improvements. The nights remained long and full of shame. The worst of it, coming off the painkillers, was seeing for the first time, with good clean eyes, the terrible despair that came with the brain injuries. It transformed people in a way the other injuries couldn't. There was a new patient called Vern who spent his days in a wheelchair and his nights upright in a body brace. I never heard him speak. One weekend his family came to visit and they decorated his bedspace and they took him around the grounds and they opened presents together and they tied balloons to his chair and they cut cake they did not eat. Later that evening one of the balloons slipped free and bounced into the corner of my little view onto the ceiling, and I watched it there while it rutted and emptied and finally sank away. The papers were always talking up the centre as this great place of hope and potential and new beginnings but there was an ugliness to it too and, as in life, the ugliness was shut away into shadows and corners and forgettable places because, seeing the awful suffering of the living, how could we, the young and the healthy and the happy and the passed over, how could we possibly go on? When I think back to that place now, when I'm reminded of the hopelessness, I think of a balloon come free, deflating in a sorry corral of ceiling. Of not being able to turn away.

It wasn't long after Kyle started walking again that a couple of military charities got together to provide a fund for his fiancé, allowing her to take a sabbatical and move to a small studio flat nearby. She began visiting every day. It did a lot of good for me, having her there, the muddle and play of an outsider, overhearing her brightly persistent family talk sustained without flag or cynicism, and as the weeks ran I accumulated a bank of junk detail that, in its own way, afforded me a feeble kind of intimacy. What would Jackie say about the conservatory when she got back? Was uncle Ernie ever going to visit the GP about his fucking ulcers? The days quickened like this, and the quickening of the days seemed somehow to portend the quickened refashioning of my broken body. I could play headgames with myself like a pro.

Kyle took it differently. Without whatever downtime he needed between visits to get him back to that good place, that good dumb perky place full of hope and forget, Kyle soon bottomed out. During her visits he'd be quiet and dismissive. Kind of lumpen, a counterweight to all her unconscious energy. She was wonderfully patient and practical with him, barely knocking off a half-glance at his self pity, as though to acknowledge it would be to afford it a legitimacy all out of cant with its cause. And always *doing*, always the doing, always with one eye fixed on some tomorrow: reading him reviews of the restaurants they would visit in the autumn and tracking down pirate copies of the latest US drama serials and interrogating bricks of holiday brochures to tally up each destination against some volubly hypothetical stage of recovery the following year. True to form he'd be black when she was gone. But late in the evenings, having bled his stumps and walked his lonely lines, he would sometimes get this rare shine on him again. Rare like noticing it might be enough to fuzz it. Rare like a part of him from before. I knew when he'd got that way whenever he started tossing paper balls across the room into my neck brace (three points for any that collected *swiiiish*, two for rebounds off my face *the FUCK*). Late one afternoon he stumped his way over to my bed. Began to cover my face with playing cards and a keyring and a banana and other bedside flotsam, arranging the pile with studious care, and me laughing the whole time – hey, watch it buddy, don't you even think about it, don't you dare, leave me alone you cyborg spider-legged motherfucker – only finishing when a mound of junk towered high out of my brace that I couldn't shake even by jawing off the muscles on my face. The sister found me buried like that a half hour later and screeched holy damnation at him. That was that night I realised he was almost done with the ward.

It was late July when the head doc gave Kyle the all-clear, and preparations were made to move him through the main rehabilitation wing. It was an old joke that they knew you were good and healthy and right in the head when you started moaning about what a shithole the place was.

Back then, before all the investment and the fundraising money started rolling in, our swimming physio classes had patients bussed out to a local leisure centre with the late-morning swimmers. These classes were usually earmarked for lads further through the system, but occasional invites were extended to those on the neuro ward due to make the move across into the mainstream. Kyle had got the nod for his first visit. (I was still some way off getting the metal pulled from my legs). That was him, done: he talked me through his strokes on the Monday and Tuesday, picking over strategies to offset the drag of his stumps and his altered centre of gravity – else I'll end up collecting plasters and pubeballs off the tiling – and it got him talking about his water polo, and about two of his old training buddies, and about his scholarship, and he was later warm with his fiancé so that she became quiet and then loose and then chatty and then quiet and embarassed-sounding in the full arc of her surprise.

On the Wednesday the sister helped him pack his towel and shorts and she wheeled him out to the waiting transport. The ward was large and quiet without him. The nurses turned the beds on their rounds and the cleaner ran the vacuum through without acknowledging me. I listened to the spring rain slatting the far bank of windows. Considered lunch. Gone eleven there was a disturbance out in the corridor: a fluster of movement and voices that broke the pondsurface calm in the room. Shits and Rio were in a fury. Can you *believe* those civvie cunts? they were saying, and their anger was hot and infectious, and I asked them what happened? and Shits explained how they had gone into the main pool like always yeah (his voice all smoothness and surfaces so his anger was richly seamed with understatement), and how, considerate and quiet, they had been shuttled over to the far corner where a small area had been roped off for the physio, and how, like always yeah, they had been at their exercises when one of the mothers from the parent and toddler class at the opposite end had complained to the lifeguard, and then to management, that the soldiers' injuries were scaring the children (fuck *off*, I was saying, my disbelief also hot and infectious) and how the instructors had finished the session early and ushered them away, and how this is the thanks we get for chucking our legs away fighting their poxy fucking wars, the civvie *cunts*… The violence of our injuries worked so often to break us apart, to glug us downwards each into our personal little plughole-spirals of doubt and guilt and despair. But that day I remember there was this togetherness in our outrage that we savoured like starving men. Kyle said nothing the whole time and in the evening he refused to get out of bed to work the training bars. No paper balls looping into view on my highside letterbox panoramic.

Later that night, sometime between the waking fits on the ward, he called over to me. He said there were some things that couldn't be changed, weren't there? and I was only one open eyeball out of my sleep and I figured he was just turning over what had happened at the pool that day, making the sort of grand stupid talk that only ever holds any weight in those shapeless hours before dawn, and I told him not to be stupid, that it didn't pay to think stupid stuff like that through in the night, to go to sleep, and he was calm and controlled and his voice had a steady elegance to it that I didn't like one bit, coming back at me out of the dark again saying, maybe, maybe there are things beyond our fixing, maybe there are things set permanent, maybe? And that was all he had said and he had said it to me in such a way that I had nothing to reply, not then nor for a long time after. In the night there were screams and terrible smells and singsong cries for mummy and Sister Nikita tended us closely and without pity and then the morning came.

Kyle broke things off with his fiancé only three or fours days before he was moved through to the rehabilitation wing. It was just another thing for us not to talk about.

I worked hard and I made steady improvements. Got my eyes back. By the time I was strong enough to graduate across to rehab Kyle had already been badged up and packed off to his new life. I understood why he never came back to say goodbye. I was ok with that. None of us wanted to be reminded of what it was we had left behind.

Things were very different on the wing. The soldiers spoke openly about their injuries, and they spoke of them with coolness and detachment: single amputations dismissed as *nicks* and *flesh wounds*; disabilities of varied shape and severity referred to with all the huffed resignation of bad weather forcing a sudden change of plans. The camaraderie and the meanness and the fierceness was all there. There was hope, too. I knew of guys who spunked their entire compensation payout on sports cars with comedy registration plates (L3G L355 and TAL18AN) and on converting whole rooms into home cinemas and on monumental transnational benders, and these acts had been stupid and life-affirming, and these two so very close together that finally I came to suspect there may be many good things in life withheld from those who look it over too closely or with too earnest an eye.

I remember staying up late drinking tea and talking shit with the others about what we wanted to do with ourselves a year or two down the line and laughing ourselves sick at Vince 'Butch' Bucera who had big plans on getting himself back to the Arghandab Valley in the spring to claim satisfaction from the men who stole his arm and his continence and his short-term memory. I remember the girls that came to shoot pool with us midweek. I remember how, to a man, the old-timers would shake our hands and buy us beer and how they would turn away and swing their heads sorrowfully at the pitiless turn of the world. I remember wheelchair basketball in the sports hall. The excellent ache in my arms and shoulders and the flat timbre of the ball echoing hollow off the skylights, the smell of hot rubber smoking my palms. I remember working out in the gym with the late afternoon light on my face and bodytiredness sitting deep in me so that I was raw and lean to only those essential parts and burning to live.

Those were good days.

We would wish them back.

wake suddenly into blackness, into nighttime that blots my eyeballs, that gluts my nostrils and my ears and my throat: the vision of it slips easily from my memory like a handprint from skin or a waft on a quick breeze and trying to hold to it, to fix only some scanty portion, seems to hasten its very unmending again into that blackness that bears me within it like a drowned man, the fragments whorl and dissipate at my fingernails (purple rot; gleaming slendernesses) and though it flies me, coy to scrutiny as sleep itself, the sensation of it lingers: its absence is profound, it has weight and shape and aspect, it is defined in its very lack like a bootprint laid in newly frozen snow and the memory of it is there in the strength of my heart in my chest and the coldness of my skin against the bedsheets: it is horror (and what to make anyway of the things that visit us unbeckoned in our beds? shouldn't any right thinking man dismiss them with that same indifference with which we brushed aside souls and pixies and devils, as cognitive effluence, sparky synapsial hiccups, the stuff alone of children and new age truthseekers and hack writers? or should we revere them as portents of deeper subterannean currents, flares hung like chinese lanterns over dark and uncharted water, as hieroglyphs perhaps to read the secrets of our own true hearts?) and it was that day we left to attend a reception in the city and down in the entrance hall was a plaque for the great war that we admired for a short while, and afterwards we sat up on the balcony above the noise of the traffic with the first taste of spring in our mouths and we were buffed and shined and scrubbed pink and square and trim in our uniforms and there was a good feeling and the gentle sparkling sound of glasses touching, and bonzo was stood there by the platters talking to some guests in black tie, expressive and earnest he says to them: in memory of those who fell, that's better somehow, don't you think? it sounds accidental, almost like a stumble; have you ever considered how they laid down their lives or they paid the ultimate sacrifice never quite ring right? this just seems truer somehow, a happier fit, it's difficult to explain but you get where I'm coming from, and the men nodded politely and the women fingered the stems of their champagne flutes and I turned out to watch the river across the way and the river making a hard, broken pattern in the trees and I felt a kind of sickness in me, knowing what it had done to him, knowing that he was many nights without sleep or rest and that a familiar old part of him had become savage and vindictive and that it snapped at him unceasingly like a mad dog, knowing, with an acuity that had all the certainty of a thing heard or saw or touched, that he was coming undone, that it would ruin him and that there was no reason to it and that the war ruined us or it spared us with equitable indifference, and watching that broken play of water through the branches then it came back to me like a holy vision, sudden and complete, formed again out of blackness: the sound of the bullets as they spot the welcome ripeness of my belly, like pebbles into stagnant water, many hundreds of them to do unspeakable violence to my frail flesh one after another they pierce me, I bulge, sallow-skinned, expectant with metal and death, but wait: how I pluck them from me with delicate fingertips, how they are transformed, become slender and glassy and amethyst purple and how they glisten like cut gemstones as they turn in a slippy suck of skin, and how I gather them to me, how I hoard them, how I bear them to the light, and I know then that the tells of the strength of my heart on my ribcage and the wetness of the sheets sprang not from some distant forgotten horror, but from tenderness, from nostalgia, from love, and if this is a rune to my secret self then I do not want it read; I do not want to hear the libel of my own heart; and so I drain my glass and I watch the broken pieces of the river scatter in the wind and soon after I leave

Down in the bay that year the spring tides brought the water high up over the car park and across the road and it was good to sit among the diners on the waterfront and drink and listen to the waves sighing black against the palisade. He wrote to Marty often during that time, and he would write about the way the lights on the waterfront lit up the water and made it shine black like oil and he would write man, that was really something, you should have seen it.

When he had first come home his mother had pressed him to stay for a week or two but he had thought about all the hands he would have to shake and all the smiles and the well-wishing and all the awkward unasked questions sitting there invisible or, worse, dragged out into the light, like the way their neighbour had leaned over the wall, looked him straight and said, you must have seen some terrible things (what do you say to something like that?) and he had packed a duffel bag and taken a sleeper train out of Paddington and his mother had cried but said she understood and there was also a secret and unacknowledged relief because she had not recognised something in the way his eyes had looked.

He was staying in a room in a hostel halfway up the hill that rose out of the bay. The room was clean and functional with a low sloping ceiling and views looking back up the hill. In fine weather he could make out wheatfields bright and dusty over the rise and when the rain came in the way the macrocarpa trees leaned and twisted into the kindness of the hillface was otherworldly and calming and beautiful in a way you couldn't put words to. Something out of dream or fairytale. A ghosted childhood memory.

In the evenings he liked to drink at the bar. The local beer was very good and seemed to capture something about the way the air tasted and the smell of the sea and how the light worked on the water. It was one of those drinks you could never try back home or anywhere else without killing that special quality. He fell in with a crowd of backpackers on one of those first nights.

You drinking on your own?

Uh huh.

That's weird. You always drink on your own?

Shrug. Not always.

Right. So you like your own company?

I guess so.

Want a drink?

Sure, why not.

They were a good crowd: they drank well and without complication and quickly gave up asking him about work and home (you know, studied for a while, did some odd jobs to help out the old man, nothing all that exciting really) except to wonder out loud why *someone like you* would come *all this way* to sit alone at a bar and drink and tap your feet to the Beach Boys and Dylan and the Stones and do *jack shit*? They convinced him to sign up to the surf school down on the beach and after the first lesson the next day he went immediately to the woman at reception and booked his room for another five weeks (um…we're gonna need a deposit for that, westcountry drawl) and called his mother to give her the news. The backpackers said he was crazy and bought him a drink. That was the fourth night.

With the tide the way it was that month the surf was very good. On the best days the waves came through in strong clean lines from the groundswell and he learned to catch them while they were unbroken and blue, paddling down the face of the wave until he felt the board hitch and the nose drop and he was able to pop up and ride through with the water crashing and rushing in on itself over his shoulder. On those days the sun coming off the water made it blindshine like mercury and he would sit outback with the weight of the waves rolling unbroken beneath him and the salt crystals making stars in his eyelashes and every moment felt edged on some unspoken triumph.

Then there were the hard days when the offshore storms and the wind moved into the bay. The wind turned the waves into mess. The surf would blow itself out in row after row of white water that would hit hard and indiscriminate and empty itself of its fight all at once so that it finally sagged up against the shoreline in an exhausted froth. He never made it outback and spent his mornings wiping out in the waist-high breakers. It was a hard discipline. In the evening they would drink heavily and laugh and gripe about the way the wind had torn up the waves. But he liked the way the foam crackled and fizzed and blew across the board like it never did when the surf was clean, and the way the grey sea touched the grey sky so the horizon just got sucked up and vanished into in all that greyness, and the way his body felt empty and elated afterwards. There was something strange and intimate about the sea when it was raging like that, the same way there was an intimacy in watching someone lose their self-control to their temper.

That was the way it was early that summer. The days passed. Time did its thing. The tips of his fingers and toes went white from the saltwater and the sun burned the colour out of his hair and there was that telltale band of brown skin above the nape of his wetsuit collar. One day he looked himself in the mirror and thought he saw his face as a face that told no stories. The thought of it made his heart run.

Marty. – Pause – Jesus. Hey. How are you? I mean, how are things?

It's good to hear your voice mate. Me? Yeah, I'm good. Doing ok I guess. The doc says they'll have me fitted up in a few weeks and then there's a hell of a lot of work to get through after that. But who knows? Maybe getting a few marathons under my belt this time next year, right? Laughter. It sounded like a well-worn joke.

Pause.

Listen Marty, I should have called already. And I wanted to come visit. I really did. But I had to get away from things back home for a while, you know?

Don't even worry about it.

It's been good for me. You know. To straighten my head out or whatever.

Don't even worry about it. I understand. I really do. And thanks for all the emails and postcards. It sounds great out there. I mean it. Always good to hear about what's going on outside these same old four walls. – Laughing – Get this right, the boys on the team sent me out a huge poster of this topless chick, signed and everything, and this picture's so big right it near enough fills the far wall and each titty's about as big as my head. So anyway, me mam comes in one day and she sees this and she almost does a double-take straight out of the room and she gives me this look like I'm six again and she says, Martin (so I know I'm in the shit), she says Martin, young man, I wouldn't care if you were just *three fingers and an eyeball* sitting there in that bed right now, there is no way on God's green earth I'm letting you have that filth up on your wall. And she tears the thing up right in front of me, right on the spot. I'm there and I'm spitting feathers, properly spitting, but at the same time I'm thinking to myself, you just can't fault a woman for logic like that, huh? Woe fucking betide a pair of good honest titties.

Ha. Sounds like your old lady alright.

Yeah. Sometimes I think she's got about enough fight in her to put me back together for good. Laughter: quieter, shorter.

Pause.

Listen mate. I've got a big ask. I was thinking maybe I could come down to where you are for a few days. The doc says it'll do me good to get out and take on some of that coastal air you've been gobbing off about. Mam thinks she's found a place we can stay nearby.

Of course. – Pause – You have to. I've got tons to show you. How soon can you get down?

I don't want to cause you any trouble.

Don't even kid. No, definitely. You have to.

How are you looking for the end of the month?

He met the girl early into the third week. She was a bright kid: young but already smart enough not to ask too much. He knew plenty of people who could learn a thing or two from her. When they put the fireworks on up at the clifftops she saw what happened to his eyes when the first rockets went off and the cordite fumes began to curl up in the torchlight and she took his hand and led him back to the hostel. They spent the night together with a half-finished bottle of Havana Club at the foot of the bed and in the morning she leant into the soft part of his shoulder as they walked along the cliffs and she told herself that she could feel the weight and the tension gone out of him. He said nothing when she moved her backpack into his room the next day.

In the evenings they would sit and share a joint and watch the sun burning out on the horizon, strips of soft luminous red glowing through the cloud and black skiffs silhouetted in the distance and the smell of salt on the breeze and the stickiness of the salt on their hands and faces. They liked to talk about the way the surf had been. They talked about the backpackers and her girlfriends back home and how the weed took the hardness out of things. And they talked in irresistible untruths about a future beyond the bay even though both knew, somewhere in that silent instinctive place, that their only future was that contained within that moment on the clifftops. One lost second stretching out into forever: the day bleeding away into its mirrored self and the skiffs parked out there fixed and sentinel with the world about them pooling to fire. The cool wind rushing away over the surface of the water, stirring the sandgrass between their toes.

When it was time for her to leave they shared a long kiss down in the lobby and they promised each other to stay in touch but she could already feel that something had come down between them. Even as she was driving up out of the bay she could feel the first twinges of disgust, of having been used in some way that she couldn't place, and she embraced the disgust and called him something filthy under her breath. And she embraced the disgust because it covered the terrible sensation of longing that was already beginning to pull at her guts.

In the mornings he would lean out of his window and smoke and watch the early shadows leaning back up into the hill, the sun cutting at low blind angles off the dew. Afterwards he would join the others in the water and when the weather was good they would work on the righthanders that peeled off the reef at the foot of the cliffs. Solid four or five footers on the best days (fuckin stoked man, fuckin stoked). He spent a lot of time in the water and he learned quickly. Outback he learned to watch the humps of green rollers further out and to watch for the way a shiver of dark would flicker across their top when they were heavy and ready to break, and he learned to watch that darkness dance and flicker and turn heavy and fill the bowl with shadow, and he learned to position himself downwave so he was sitting snug in the pocket at the moment the peak turned white and began to tumble. You lost everything in the violence of the best waves. He thought that was kind of funny.

It was the fourth week. Marty came down on the Friday and they arranged to meet in a café on the waterfront. The café was quiet and sandblown and outside it was overcast. Marty arrived and his mam had to help lift the front of the wheelchair over the lip of the doorframe, a waitress apologising too much and moving chairs to one side. There was a tartan blanket over the place where his legs had been. He thought he had steadied himself for seeing Marty this way but having it all there before him, the awful way the blanket sank empty against the frame of the chair, made him hold down a gasp. Something rolling over in his belly. He hated himself for that. Marty was wasted down to his cheekbones and jawline and his smile drew the softness of his face into hollows, the shirtcollar hanging loose on his neck. It was all wrong. An obscenity. Marty had always had this dumb earthy strength to him, like a bull or an old tree or a thick slab of hill. Had made living like something simple and artless and kind. He had figured Marty's injury would somehow have toothpaste-squeezed all that strength into the rest of him, into broad shoulders and broad arms and bright bright eyes. It had taken enough already. It had no fucking right to anything else.

So. I lose my pins and *I'm* the one travelling two hundred miles to see *you*? Marty laughed and pulled him down into his chair and the two embraced tight until they squeezed the breath out of each other. His mam excused herself to buy a paper.

You look good mate. Honest you do. He thought he heard his voice catching.

I've been worse I guess. The surgeons did a good job on me. The doc says I'm healing quickly. Get to test drive my prosthetics in a few weeks. Should be up and about pretty soon with a bit of luck. Girls love a war wound or three, right?

Is it still hurting?

Hardly ever. Although you should see me try and scratch my fucking ankle man. That's a killer. I'm there on my back leaning round to touch the end of my bed scratching fucking thin air and there's this guy, Rio, and he's in the next bed along with his left arm blown off and orange minetape wrapped around the cubicle just to freak out visitors and VIPs even though it makes his girlfriend cry to see it, and he's watching me itching and squirming and he's all like, hey Marty you fuck, hows about I scratch your fucking ankle with my fucking hand? That's a killer.

The waitress came by and cleared up a single cup of coffee gone cold.

I'll come and visit you soon, I promise. I'm going to wallpaper your room with so many tits your mum'll have a heart attack.

I'll hold you to that. But hey, enough of this me-me-me shit. How are you doing? Looks like you've got yourself a nice little bolthole here. Out of season at least.

It's ok. Does the trick.

Pause.

I spoke to JB last week. He said they hadn't heard from you since you got back. Said you'd gone cold on them.

Shrug. You know how it is. Living out of each other's pockets like that all the time. I just needed to catch some space for a while.

Marty nodded slow-time. He flipped a drinks coaster off the edge of the table with the back of his hand and caught it. And again, twice over. Outside the sail on an ice cream stand was banging in a sand cloud.

So you going to show me around or what?

Shit, I don't even know where to start. I've got to introduce you to the guys up at the hostel. You'll like them.

I want to surf.

Pause.

Are you serious?

The next day a squall blew down off the cliffs into the bay and up into the hills. It left the bay clean and polished and raw. Afterwards the sky had that dazzling minted quality of freshly laid snow. Marty stripped himself down to his shorts and unwound the elasticated bandages from his legs. There was an enflamed pink jigsaw pattern across the end of the stumps where the staples had been. It was an ugly look: thick and bulging and roughshod. He caught it in quick glances while he tore off the plastic wrapping on the bodyboard they had haggled from a store on the front. He looked Marty in the face.

Ready?

He lifted Marty up onto his back and there was a brief sickening instant when he felt the lightness of him on his shoulders before he was able to recover himself.

He jogged them down to the water, the sound of his feet slapping against the wet sand. It was early in the morning. There were a couple of surfers testing out the break beyond the point and seabirds ankle-splashing the river runout and overhead two lone stripes of jet wash on the cleanness of the sky and very little else.

He ran them into the surf whooping with the chill of the waves numbing his toes and splashing between his legs. He ran them out until the water was at his belly, came to a dead halt, and put Marty headfirst over his shoulders into the water. Marty came to the surface with a gasp, grinning and spitting saltwater and treading the water with his arms. It was wonderful to see him that way. In the dark of the water he looked whole and strong. He handed Marty the board and lined him up with the nearest wave and pushed him off as it crashed through. The first waves upended him so that he rolled under and came up spitting and ragged, but soon enough he was hollering and taking long clean lines into the shore with the surf against his thighs. And each time he would wade in to the point where Marty had beached in an inch of water and swing him onto his back and run them out again. There was that same happy exhaustion he knew from a hard surf and they stayed in the water until their fingers marbled red and blue with cold.

After one wave he found Marty lying there on his back at the very edge of the surf, and Marty was looking up into the sky and smiling with his arms making angel impressions into the sand and he said wow, you can really forget a whole lot out here, huh?

On Marty's last night they went out on the cliffs and drank bottles of cold beer, piling the empties up in an old cardboard crate and tossing cigarette butts onto the rocks. The breeze coming off the bay was cool and fresh and they caught snatches of music blown over from a campfire blinking on the far side.

They were quiet for a while. He lit a cigarette and turned to Marty.

I've been coming here. Most evenings.

Yeah?

It's something else, don't you think?

It's nice.

I could watch the sea for hours like this. I bet it's got a whole lot of stories to tell. That's what I always think when I'm sat up here long enough: I bet it's got stories to tell. But it never does. It keeps on raging or pawing or whatever it needs to do, but it always keeps its secrets. – Laughing – Suppose you get to thinking this kind of crazy shit if you spend too much time in your own company, huh?

Marty drained his beer off and dumped the empty and cleaned a new one. Don't I know it.

I'm glad you came, though. Really.

Yeah, me too. And the doc was right after all. This fresh air has made me a new man.

He laughed to himself as if party to some private amusement and then he looked up and the two of them swapped clumsy kid smiles and then they turned out to the water and the low sun.

Pause.

Do you ever think about what happened?

All the time. Only it's funny. I can remember everything that happened down to the smallest detail, right? I can remember a fly sort of pirouetting on my shoulder, turning in a neat circle just here where my collar bone touches my shoulder. I can see the stitching of the cotton and the pattern of the camouflage and this little fly doing his little dance; I can remember Daz shouting mega sarcastic and angry-like – putting on a voice – *will someone please get the fucking point-five onto that position*, and he's just peeping over the top of the ditch he's in, all dinner-plate eyes like one of them characters out of an old Warner Brothers cartoon; I can remember the smell of the dirt. I can remember that very clearly. And I can remember everything afterwards. It's only the middle I'm missing.

He took a long drag on his cigarette. He was looking into the bay.

Suppose I should be thankful for small mercies. – Blowing the smoke out over his head – Only the thing is, I can remember all this, the before and after, but it's like they're not really my memories at all. More like a photo album I know really well or a film I've seen a hundred times over. Does that make sense? I can see the outlines and the colours but none of it means anything. It's kind of funny. The way things work out I mean.

Pause.

It's different for me. I remember everything that happened perfectly. Real clarity to it. It reminds me of when I was a kid and I broke my ankle playing football. Even after all these years, when everything else is all faded and forgotten like you're looking back on it with chlorine in your eyes, even after all this time I can still picture that moment my ankle snapped, the sound and the look of the way it twisted round on itself and the feeling I had after, everything bright and sharp. That's the way it is for me now. When it comes back it's all there like it's happening right in front of me. Every time.

They fell quiet again. The light was going out behind the fields and the shoulder of the hill and there was a clean, metallic freshness from the the dayheat sweating out of the grass.

You know it's not your fault, don't you? Marty said.

He had to look away. He found himself chewing his tongue to hold it all down inside of him. He was thinking about the ghosts that came out to play when he closed his eyes at night. He was thinking about how they liked to race around his room and laugh and blow the shadows off the curtains and onto the walls. And he was thinking of the things they whispered to him.

You know none of this was your fault. – Marty slapping his stumps and pulling at some grass and tossing it into the breeze – It wasn't your fault. It wasn't my fault. It wasn't anyone's fault. Things just happen. Our hands got dealt and we did what we could with what we were given. You can't go around carrying all this on your shoulders. It's not yours to carry. Give it up.

Out in the bay the lights from the waterfront were making the water shine black like oil. *Man, that was really something, you should have seen it.*

He sat outback in a lull. His legs dangled into the water with the board rocking gently side-to-side, the heavy weight of a maybe-wave rolling underneath. The sunlight made a sandbar beneath him peer up green through the water. Wow. You can really forget a whole lot out here, huh? He was waiting for a wave. There was only the horizon and the waiting.

a better man could have made the desert dawn to come again: could have put the dry cold there in your throat and shaped the mountains into wholeness out of bluely yielding night, could have undone that blackness once more into a sky that is height without limit and so flawlessly impossibly clear that it cheats you into thinking that, knowing where to look, you might read the complexions of planets and systems turned to you in their outflung orders, could somehow have shown it to you both in the snowflake singularity of that morning and as a portent blazing with universal significance, the moment of creation itself playing out over and over into eternity, and made you know fear and trembling rightly before it; a better man would have brought the people to you whole, in song and balm and stripe, with painterly judicious care he would unshroud them from their many obscurities: the caravans of kuchi nomads who roam their gauntly flocked cattle like penitents through foothills and flood plain and unending inconsolable desert, and remote cabals of pashtun that live as their distant ancestors before them, mannered in such ancient shapeless customs they have almost shed from themselves entirely the pettinesses of creed and ritual, become almost tribed of sand and clay alone, and of the barakzai khans that mediate over the verdancy of the irrigated country and the sharecroppers in the fields squatted impassively into their upflexed heels, blackeyed and cunning like eagles, and the sayeds standing yet their fierce and faithful watch over the tomb of mir salim, and the modest nobility of the hazara and the baluchi of the southern ranges and the battle-thirsty uzbek clans and every other tongue and tribe that goes to redden the courseways of those wild provincial bloodlines, knowing that within them is all else and that the story of the people is also the story of the land and of the invader and of the war; a better man would have told of the men who flew into battle winged to their helicopters and doing so he would subtly unpick the banal mechanisms by which incident becomes legend, and he would have spoken of the black days of the IED fields and the many field amputees, limbs hung like fruit pendulous and char and overripe in the branches, and of the down's child they detonated at the head of the patrol and where I see only desolation without horizon he would have discovered in it all some hidden dignity and a hope that was not false and a lesson, and in that he would have showed, without flourish or two-bit trickery, how meaning can be derived truly from that which has no meaning; in a phrase he could have called the richness of the city night into your nostrils, naan dough crisping on open tandoors and the blown-cinder smells of a people that live and commune and arbitrate by fire, a wind fragrant with coarse desert sands, he could have strung the backroads again in those pretty electric ball lights at ramadan and made you to feel their colours on your cheeks, made you know that feeling that was almost sanctuary, almost heartsickness, deep in the pitchy nighttime unknown of a doorless shopfront or a stall under canvas; a better man would have told of the simple boyish thrill when the first enemy mortars fell, the whooping and the high fives and the fuck-mes, and he would have made it not boyish nor a thing of disgrace but he would have afforded it a significance and a curiosity deserving of all human action, dispassion informed by compassion, and by that same measure he would not have shied from the great joy that is often there in the fighting or the profound sense of belonging among men that have tasted the dirt together and shared whispered godless oaths under sheets of fire for he today that sheds his blood with me shall be my brother, yes, and from out of these multitude contradictions he would have found something small and true and forever; and he would do all this without embellishment and with the right words, the only words, the necessary words, and the austerity of it would be an indignation against the sated silent consciences of men, and he would do this without recourse to bitterness or pride or sentiment, with a coldness of eye he would extinguish himself from the world of his creating and the things he speaks would achieve a truth beyond the brief flame of their being; a better man than I would animate them again in the wonderful imperfections of their bodies, oh god to puff breath into long-stilled chests and speak joyful curses once more upon stiff tongues: to salvage yet a little life from history, for history is the very falsification of life and it would deny us everything...

but it is late and the light fades and I am not equal to my work; there are only these pieces left to me, scattered and disordered and incomplete, troubled orphan memories that find no solace in the grand old stories nor in the many peddled sacrifices and noblenesses of boyhood nor in the witting promises of men of power (nor even fulfilment in the pacifist's poetry, whose words cohere at least in the graceful consensus of their disgust); I am as an old man sorting fragments of newspaper from a shoebox, yellowed cuticled photographs shed from their chronology, a clutch of diary pages dimmed by cloudy eyes, hoping perhaps to discover in it all some modest consolation, some pale symmetry that they might finally be soothed in their torment, that they might be laid to rest; and in the falling night they are there with me still: the women that stand and weep at the roadside and an afternoon when the men forgot themselves in song and woody wringing his hands over the deskwork like some worried old maid and a dead man on a slab that gets in my clothes all sweetness and coalbrick and cooked fat and a moment out there on the plains with the artillery wailing down upon us that reveals itself to me like an epiphany on the twooneeight from croydon one blowy saturday afternoon and a shadow that is there with me always: dressed in the gathering gloom they clamour about me like beggars, feverish, insistent, vivid with that surprising gasp of light from a candleflame at the point of going out they beseech – speak us once more that we might not be lost

I

The gate shut. The street noise gave way to a sudden insulated silence that echoed up between the high square walls of the compound. An insect chattered in the grass. You would not have believed such a place of quiet could exist in the city had you not seen it for yourself. The walls were shaded and grey and dark at the corners with the varicose stain of dead ivy and the sun fell flat on the cemetery garden where rangy trees potted the chalk paths run between the ruin of old gravestones and the memorial plaques stood neatly at the far end. Sheep in limp grey wool grazed beside the stones. It had been a beautiful day. You made your way over to the terracotta shed in the corner where the old man Rahimullah was brushing two sheep away from the doorframe and leaning against the twisted shape of his cane. You handed him five dollars and he looked up at you and nodded and chewed his gums. His face all cracked and sunken like the soil. An infant's bright, glassy eyes.

In the courtyard there were rows of square plots sunk into moss and drygrass and many white headstones and nubs of crumbled white rock and plaques that had bleached the colour of sandstone with all the detail washed out of them. One of them read In Sacred Memory Of, breaking abruptly into a sandsmoothed tear where the plaque had worked itself away into the contours of the wall. Fresh petals scattered at the base of Aurel Stein's headstone and a clump of chewed stalks. Ancient graves of explorers and aid workers and hippies (Billy Batman loves Joan, Jade, Hassan, Caldoania and Digger written out in buoyant chunky serif typeface; a small heart scribbled off-centre; a gesture of defiance and oblivion captured in a single kite-shaped slab) and merchants and colonial soldiers that put you in mind of the old Kipling verse about the Afghan women coming out to cut up the soldiers' remains. The stones and the plaques against the far wall boasted clean edges and mottled marble textures and the names were cut in deep hollow strokes. Bright rings of poppies with regimental badges lay stacked up against them. ISAF. German. Polish. Spanish. Italian. American. Campaign honour rolls.

And then. And then. The first of the black British tablets was centralised at the furthermost wall of the garden. The spill of names, each in distinct blocks of gold lettering, had created an overflow so that an additional two tablets had begun a clockwise creep at the edges where the rose bushes grew. You read, slowly. Many of the early names meant nothing. A paean to ignorance and innocence and a half-caught glimpse of a self you had once known. On the second tablet there were the names that put a sudden breath into fragments of old memory that fluttered up unsolicited from the deep place where they had settled, like that of an old girlfriend's perfume or a song from a summer in your youth: the strong canvas smells and the patterns of the lamp on the tented walls when you had learned Scouse Brady had been killed (Buster catching the way you looked early and asking, you gonna be alright there buddy); the time back home drinking with big Al Henderson when you heard about the ambush and you had solemnly raised your glasses and how afterwards the alcohol had made it feel showy and insincere; the way that young Sapper had died and how you had known then, instantly and with a conviction that took you by surprise, that there are deaths beyond redemption and beyond the comfort of a padre's well-meaning ascription to the old lie *he died doing what he loved*; Billy Tait's funeral with his fiancé standing at the altar and this look of poison on her face, spitting through her tears, was it worth it? I don't know. I just don't know.

There was the soft call of a starling unseen and the stones

showing vivid in the last of the light. You opened your bag and you took out the small woodenframed photograph and you rested it upright against the base of the first tablet and you stood back two paces and you crossed your wrists at the waist and you stood and you stood.

II

Returning to Kabul for the last time you found the city a different place. The dust and the shit that had hung in the air during the summer months had finally settled against the coolness of the roads and the whitewashed walls and the rutted alleyways that capilliaried across the old town and above it all the air so thin and crystalline it almost quivered and you could see all the way out to the northernmost mountains suddenly broken open dark and snowcreased and pristine where they stood up into the sky along the bowl of the horizon, and there the city in the cool winds of the dying summer was like Lazarus after they rolled the stone away.

You had seventy-two hours in-country for the handover. Three months and you were out for good. Tick tock. On the first day you met with the incoming commander and briefed the Special Forces team on operations across the AO and you shared a cold beer with the boys down in the Snake Pit and you span them the old cliché about their time too rolling around faster than they could imagine that always sounded like bullshit to those left behind and an unspoken gasp of regret to those soon to go. That evening you called Khalid. He spoke in the precise, measured notes of schooled RP and an expensive English university education, but there was something in the delay he took composing his sentences, a slightness of breath as he put shape to the words, that spoke of his delight. You made plans to meet the next day. Neither of you gave voice to the assumption that this was the last time you would ever see each other.

In the morning you watched the street vendors from your window while you washed. You watched them sweeping sheets of shopfront water out into the gutters, the sweet biley guttersmells swelling and steaming up over the basin and condensing into breathy clouds against the glass. Shot through with the freshness of the early morning those smells took on a beauty that was all their own. The change in the city was all around you. Walking out onto the streets you could feel it in the way the sun warmed your forearms and the back of your neck like it had never done in the close grey heat of the summer. Clean. Sharp. There was the mini-mart with the buzz of LEDs blinking Happy All The Time over the doorframe and the steam coming off the wet black pavement and the bawl of Bollywood radio from the kitchen where you could taste the haze of old kebab grease in the air as the griddles burned into life. A gang of street kids skittered along behind you in oversized tatty pink flip-flops toting for change. Days gone you had taken to tossing a dollar to the girl with the big green eyes and the fingers that were tapered to claws and black to the knuckle from frostbite. The runners had caught on quickly and pressed her to hustle you for bigger money and you had just smiled and asked her something asinine like shouldn't you be at school? and she would smile back up at you with those eyes glowing, not understanding but understanding, and the other kids skipping and hollering around you and flashing looks of confusion and disappointment at each other the time you had handed out cereal bars and biros from your day sack.

You followed your old daily route where it took you through the ballast checkpoint into what the papers back home were calling the green zone of the city. The hand-smoothed pumice of the stucco walls built tall either side and the sounds and colours of the street dropping away behind you until you were left with only the quiet and the tiny lightfooted birds splashing in the places where the sprinklers span and beds of papery rock-rose flowered like crepe streamers out of the dirt. There was the maimed old mule that slept outside the Ambassador's residence, stretching out in the heat with its tail twitching against the flies that clouded the gentle heave of its ribs and flank. Ahead there was the junction in the road. Old memories. Blind drunk on the way back from the embassy cocktail party, pistols made ready stuffed in the waistbands of your trousers and the dust on the road blowing silently widthways out through the railings that opened onto the abandoned playing fields. You remembered feeling charged. Invulnerable. A sense of absolute entitlement that was part drink and part the cold press of the pistol against your groin and part hard-dick colonial swagger. And one of the others pulling up short by the junction yelling out, hey, anyone hear about those contractors that got busted taking target practice out by the bazaar? – pause – and the almost-suggestion dangling there in the air between you until someone had got hold of themselves and suggested that maybe there was time for one last drink down in the Pit instead, before you called it a night, yeah? and all the craze and bluster and bombast suddenly gone out of the moment. The dust wiggling in a silent s pattern over the surface of the road.

You shook your head at the memory. It was like a bad taste, something to swallow down quickly. It was a kind of disgust that was common to you then, looking back on the things you had done and been party to, disgust that stemmed in part from the believer's faith you had put in the war effort, in the Strategy. You felt it now sharply and justly proportioned against those swaggered heights of superiority that had found perhaps their simplest expression in a sneered bootstep, in a turn of the hips calibrated finely with disdain. For a man's humility is there in plain sight in his walk. There was great shame in it, in the disgust, yes, but there was also compassion and sadness. A wry and vantaged amusement. You looked back on yourself with a shamed and forgiving heart, like you would on any fool trying to make himself from the pieces of a life yet unlived. Khalid had called it the conqueror's reward, called it a post-imperial hangover. Khalid had it nailed most of the time.

Coming up out of the passageways of the green zone you could see the great grey reaches of Kohi Asamayi skewering the city in two at its centre, the basin of blue spilling out over its summit and the soft ripple tracks of cloud vapour beating away towards the whitepeaks of the Kush ringing the horizon. There were the settlements built high into the cliff face and the red flecks of kites whirling and bobbing in combat, and below you could see the children playing out along the flats where the Olympic swimming pool was drained and dormant and the thin muzzle of the high diving board snouted over the plateau like gallows scaffolding. In days past the Taliban would march criminals and homosexuals and adulterers blindfolded off the end of the board onto the tiles below. Those who survived were judged innocent. You had always thought that a nice touch: irrational, medieval, self-parodic. You soon became indifferent to the cruelty. It was all around you and it was like a colour that you could not name, nor one you had known before, and the light it cast was foul and low-hanging and it touched everything, curling up into the most hidden and secret of places and washing boldly over the wild open plains that bore the marks of their desolation to an indifferent and unflinching universe. That colour had left its mark in peoples' eyes and in the things they said and in the ruin you saw, and it spoke of a future also defined by acts of cruelty committed by man against man. Seeing the diving board reminded you of the night the dust storm had blown into the city and how walking home alone that night there had been the sound of the dry leaves tumbling across the concrete like electricity against the blackness and the whispered rush of the coming storm that you could feel in the soles of your feet; you remembered the wild dog that had slipped out of the shadows, assuming a hesitant canter at your heels with its ears pinned back, and the way it had only slowly become sure of itself; sniffing dry-nosed at your fist, your hand running through the mats of hard pelt along its haunch until you could feel the telescope of vertebrae under your fingers; bounding in clutzy puppy lopes to return the branches you had underarmed into the ditch at the roadside. There had been a simple understanding between you. And you remembered the approach to the checkpoint, the guards pelting it with rocks and cursing while you were still a long way off, and how you had fixed your eyes and kept your stride as it disappeared out of the periphery of your sight, choking back the urge to turn around and sweep the animal into your arms and carry it away into the night. Not understanding why, but knowing it and having it there right at the core of you. The whimpering and the noises you had heard somewhere far off in the darkness. And that terrible feeling afterwards. After feeling so little for so long.

Looking back up at the diving board with the clouds inert and the whole earth rushing away beneath you and thinking about the storm and the dog and the things that had happened that night, you knew then that the cruelty would be there long after you were dust and dead memories, and that there was no way to explain it except to say that it had a power and a justification all of its own. And sometimes that is all the reason anyone can hope for.

With the mountain at your back the valley flats shook out onto the highway that ran like a scar from the foothills and across the dead empty ground where slopwater pooled and dried and stained the white dirt in concentric rings like carbon fouling the spiral of a rifle bore, and out to where the shopfronts began spilling onto the road with the old wooden barrows curling under the weight of vegetables and rice heaped up in hessian sacking and bright primary-coloured boxes of imported wheat and candy piled roadside beneath where the burned out fairy lights swung in knotted ribbons like bunting in the wind that was tumbling through and the wind loosely cut with saffron and coriander and cardamom and the salty tongue of old fish cooking in the sun, and finally out to where the road became the city and the city growing over it and the road was lost amongst the tectonic swirl of traffic that jostled and roared and smoked and sounded a chorus of horns that would play on into the night so that with the heavy curtains drawn against the bellcurve of the room it was impossible to tell if it was dawn or dusk or any damn time in-between.

Out there at the edges, where the road fed into the lapping outskirts of the city, was the place where you had arranged to meet. They called it Chicken Street. You shuffled past the open stalls feeling yourself beaming with the naked self-consciousness of an outsider. Hands stuffed in pockets. Grateful for the anonymity of your sunglasses. While you were still a long way off Khalid had seen you and rushed to you and thrown his arms around you in a crush of body smells and fabric leeched with incense, and for a moment neither of you said anything. Only later would it occur to you that the warmth of friendship at its most elemental is indistinguishable from the warmth of forgiveness.

Let me look at you. – Fixing you by the shoulders, grinning broadly – Hmm. You look healthy. Perhaps a little paler than before. Longer hair. The beard. I'm not sure about the beard. But healthy. Good. He nodded, satisfied.

Hey, what's all this? – Patting the overhang on his buckle – Have you been putting on weight, Khale? Has Habiba been feeding you up?

Ha, you think this is bad. Habiba is fat like a courtesan. *Huge.* She is expecting. Tsk, you shouldn't be surprised to hear your old friend Khalid still takes great pleasure in the delights of the marital bed.

So. Old man Khalid is to be a father.

Inshallah. But come, come, we have much to speak about. I have made plans for us.

You stopped off and drank syrupy chai in the shade of a cafe awning and you watched the sugar and the ash fragments of tealeaf billowing with every tip of the glass. Khalid talked for much of the time and the conversation was easy and unforced and for a while you forgot the war and all those months apart seemed to collapse in on themselves into something inconsequential, something other. When you stood to leave you saw that you had torn a coaster into a pile of tiny scraps.

Some of the buildings set back from the concourse were heavily scarred or punched through with shrapnel holes that had almost closed in on themselves or bore halfmoon Soviet blastmarks that blowholed the midday sun. The streetfront itself was little changed from the hippie trail that used to snake down out of the Khyber Pass. Vendors plying sun-bleached rugs with nine-eleven and AK-47 and Operation Enduring Freedom storyboard hieroglyphs stitched in crude three-colour polygons (for you misser I give you twenty dollar, ok for you I give you for twelve, hey misser, twelve dollar, hey you look at this, fine material, very fine, ok for you seven dollar, hey misser, where you go). Small headed chickens with their feathers shiny and slick to the skin piled in crates twenty-high shrilling at you as you passed; Khalid poking at them with his fingers and laughing that strange falsetto laugh that shook out from his belly. Eyeless wolf hides laid out in rows and the fur hardened from the sun and the undersides rough and dimpled where they had been hacked away. Ornate copies of old Martini-Henry singleshot carbines that you could only tell from the messy stamps on the stock or the way the bolt snapped just slightly off-flush or how the barrel was liable to explode in your face if you were crazy enough to try firing the bastard; and Khalid pulling open the breach on the undercarriage to peer inside and saying that the copies were hand-forged up in the hills where the craftsmen would pull up railway tracks for the iron necessary for the metalwork, to which several derailments and deaths had been linked over the years, finally sneering and tossing the rifle barreldown into the basket saying they weren't worth the wood they were built with, and you thinking jesus, with a genealogy that torturous how could they not be worth every single fucking penny?

You haggled over a Kashmiri blanket and left empty-handed. You looked at your watch. It was still early in the afternoon.

Do you need to get back? Khalid asked.

Not at all. Unless you have things to see to.

I'm all yours. I cleared the whole day as soon as you called. – Pause – I've got something to show you, something I think you'll enjoy. A real treat.

Go on.

Khalid had a wicked smile on his face and he gave deliberate pause before replying, looking left to right across at the kaleidoscope of whirling tobacco smoke and gunpowder-red spices in baskets and feathers and sunlight gone mouldy in the puddles and joints of meat trussed up to the bone and children chasing between the stalls.

He licked his lips.

You could hear the roar and exhalation of the crowd on the very edges of the wind while you were still over a mile away. Khalid led you in through thin streets that shook the dust from their walls as you made the approach to the stadium. The clatter of feet stamping at the panelled benching up and down the spectator stands; the rapid, thunderous bass from within that you could feel in the soft buzz and jarring in your joints. You took your place in the north stand. Khalid shook hands with a man he introduced to you as the trainer, as if that were explanation enough. The trainer wore a thick purple overcoat despite the heat and he smiled at you cordially through a mouthful of gold teeth, the blue glass bulb of a shisha vase nestled between his knees.

At first it had been very difficult to make sense of the movement out on the pitch behind the welter of low-hanging dust rolling slow and languid and coarsely sunlit. As your eyes adjusted you could make out the heavy dark barrels of the horses threading in and out of the pack in a tight slalom with their heads snapped back and their nostrils and lips flared and their bodies coming in so close that each pass brought off small plumes of the salt and dust whitening their bellies. The riders wore heavy leather tunics and quilted greaves and turbans rolled above their ears and fixed stares that drew their cheeks in against the swell of broken teeth. You watched the pack moving like a single organism, drifting in a fixed dance over the gravel with a small cadre of riders circling the edges and the foam of horses rearing out of the centre. Lips peeled and strained necks keeling skywards.

It might seem chaotic at first, even random, Khalid said, but it is tremendously complex. The ability to hold the balance of the horse whilst pushing and pulling and circling; knowing where your teammates are and how to react to sudden shifts in strategy. At its best this is our country's finest art form. It is blood and war and subtlety and grace. Watch –

The pack had suddenly given way, almost folding in on itself: one rider dragging the goat carcass in his right hand and the other riders low against the contours of their horses in chase, flaying their necks and cheeks with sharp snaps at the elbow, and the pack swinging round to head off the rider as he broke towards the open ground. Three or four riders came in from the side. You saw the lead rider dig his heels hard into the paddles, bunch his reins at the scruff in one hand, and swing off the saddle so that he was hanging from the side of the horse: his free hand trailing the ground ready for the snatch, the horse holding the line of charge. He hit the runner at almost the same moment as the two on his flank: you saw the horse stagger crossways and then fall on its back with the rider thrown clear and almost instantly the pack reforming in a huddle that lurched left and right over the place where the horse had turned itself onto its belly and was working to its knees. The pack had spun a halfturn clockwise in a corkscrew dust cloud when you saw the fallen horse bolt for the near stand, clearing straight up through the crowds until its legs buckled on the top row and they were able to haul it in. Its pupils framed by a wide yellow-white rim of iris and blowing hard through its teeth, like something had snapped or come free.

And the trainer leaning across to you saying, they select and breed them for toughness, you understand. Calm under very great pressure. It is a surprisingly rare quality, even after many years of training. In that sense they are no different from the chapandaz themselves. At the highest levels there is the illusion of animal and rider being of a single mind and temperament. Extensions of one another. They must have very similar complements of that rare quality or the imbalance between them, however small, will make it as though the chapandaz himself is clumsy or inexperienced. – Giving a snort that became a spluttered cough that he did not bother to cover with his hands – It goes without saying that the most discerning chapandaz are extremely particular about their horses. I knew of one from Maimana who refused to ride for nearly five years until he found a colt of the right quality. It was a wonderful animal. Tartar in origin. Full of fire. He taught it to kneel, *to actually kneel*, to allow him to lean in and grab the goat from the dirt.

And how did it perform?

He is the President's own chapandaz now.

The trainer leaned back and took up the pipe from across his lap and drew on it twice and let the shisha smoke bubble up from the sides of his lips in slow curling wisps. Khalid smoked without his eyes leaving the pitch.

When they are still foals we take them and we stand them out in the sun for tens of hours at a time and we load them down with weight until they have broken completely and become something again and they have had the fear worked out of them. Then we can begin our real work with them. Something happens in the eyes when they are ready. – Drawing on the pipe again so that you could hear the water gurgling in the base as the cooling smoke pulled through – But this can only ever happen once. To animal or man. Working the fear out is an irreversible process. It has always seemed to me that whatever must happen inside to take the fear away must also somehow take away the mechanisms to cope with that fear. Because if it ever finds them again, then they are truly lost.

You nodded. You had seen it for yourself a long time ago.

This one, – shaking his head and gesturing over into the stands where the crowds were now closing in over the hole ploughed by the bolting horse – this one is finished.

You watched the pack break again, this time with one of the chapandaz leading the charge and his body so flat against the horse that the distended carcass tumbled behind in the dirt like old sacking; two teammates galloping at his phalanx and the rest of the pack tearing after them with the heads of the horses snapping back and forth against their halters, and the roar of the crowd washing north-to-south through the stands as the chapandaz pulled his horse short in a tight victory wheel that broke the chalk circle at the far end; holding aloft the stringy, headless carcass to an electric audience; the chasing pack peeling off slowly around the perimeter in a sullen canter. You looked over to where the bucked rider on the other side was still being dragged by his armpits out to where a battered peagreen ambulance had been parked up in the shade. Two boys skipping over the drag marks left by his legs in the sand as they rushed over to the place in the corner where a man was sat between his knees cooking flatbread.

The trainer had turned to you again, grinning through a faceful of smoke:

Magnificent, isn't it?

Afterwards you had bought bagged fruit from a corner stand and Khalid had taken you to his home. The evening quickening around you so you could feel the sudden cold coming off the whitewash. The neighbourhood was quiet, isolated from the grumble of traffic playing out softly to the north and east by the high builds and thin residential roads banked up in parallel grids all the way out to the diplomatic area. Inside there was the twang of a sitar playing out of one of the back rooms and richly textured Persian rugs tiled along the hallway and into the dining room (you like these? all of them handwoven, all of them, very high resolution of knots per square inch, you can tell from the shine and when you press from underneath like *this*) and at the far end a portrait of Ahmed Shah Massoud framed in chunky gold that was peeling black at the corners. The house was very cleanly swept throughout, excepting a fine layer of dust like silk that lay evenly on the floors and the walls and the ceiling, and the dust and the cough of the overhead lamps softening the edges of the room into a gently fragrant lotus lull that worked its way right inside of you. A lurch of homesickness that you could not explain that shook right through you and then was gone.

Sit, sit, he said. You set your boots by the door. Sat crosslegged at a braised walnut table richly ornate with kilim weave.

Habiba entered through a beaded curtain and set down a tray of sweet tea, the waft of meat currying in a pan swinging through after her with the splash and clack of the beads. You could see she was very far along. She refused your offer of help with the tray and tea.

Crossing her arms and sighing through a smile:

So where did he take you today? He was acting very secretive last night after your call. Like a little boy making plans to explore a forbidden building or kidnap a neighbour's pet. – Pause. Looking us slowly in turn – And why are you both filthy?

Khalid took us to see the buzkashi at Ghazi Stadium. It was stunning. It really was. I've never seen anything like it.

Oh Khale. Any excuse for a wager.

Khalid leant back into a pile of cushions, his fingers laced over his belly.

We hardly spent a thing. And it was an excellent game for a newcomer: a good score, lots of excitement. Well worth the trouble. I'm very glad we went. – Looking to you – Besides. Did you know they used to execute criminals there by firing squad? Or that they would bury adulterers up to their necks in the dirt and stone them as the half-time entertainment for a soccer match? Or that they would amputate the limbs of robbers and leave the severed arms on the ground for the crowds to gawp at when it was done? Tsk, Ghazi has a terrible, sordid history to its name. – Blowing on his glass then cracking an impish half-smile – As I see it, a little bit of gambling every now and then is a countryman's patriotic duty. An obligation of sorts. The very least we can do to celebrate and cherish these little badges of our freedom.

Bravo Khale, Habiba slow-clapped. Bravo. All very inspiring. But can I ask you not to wage your covert little crusade out of the housekeeping budget in future? What *will* I do with him, eh?

He's incorrigible, you agreed, momentarily disorientated by some oddness to their patter: the familiar snap and footwork of a couple squabbling on the most equal and intimate of footings set against the steeply antiquated, steeply patriarchal connotations of your surroundings.

Habiba returned from the kitchen carrying steaming silver trays of palao with great shining lamb cuts encrusting mounds of rice and naan toasted with poppy seeds and pickled fruits and small copper bowls filled with water. She showed you how to scoop up chunks of the rice between the tongue-wetted pads of your thumb and fingers and they laughed as you scattered rice and gravy in your beard and swung your legs out to one side and back in again to a crossed position, the small of your back in exquisite agony (I've never seen you look quite like such a foreigner she said, blushing into her fingers). By the time you had finished there were fragments of food outlining the place where you had sat; the sensation of oil and spices on your mouth and lips that remained even after you had towelled your face.

Habiba cleared the plates and retired for the evening, apologising: It was lovely seeing you again, you must write. You must.

Khalid opened a cabinet and took out a bottle and poured a thumbful each into two glasses. The wine tasted of sultanas and paraffin. It gave a strong kick so that the immediate rush and lightness behind your eyes was almost enough to mask the rolling in your stomach. You set your half-finished glass to one side. Khalid was laying back, blowing up smoke rings into the fixings.

And so. How long is it now until you begin your new life as a civilian?

Only a few weeks now. My paperwork is ready. This trip is my last operational task before the formal handover begins.

And what will you do?

I've got some work lined up with a legal team in London due to begin just before Christmas. It should be an interesting change of pace. I mean, shit, I can barely remember the last time I wore a suit for work. I'm hoping to spend more time with Jules and the girls. It's not fair for me to be away for these great long stretches anymore. They're growing up so fast. And Jules worries herself sick when I'm gone.

Hmm. It will be a difficult transition, Khalid said, raising the glass to his lips. But a necessary one. Do you feel prepared?

It's strange. A bit like leaving a family. And it's been my life for so long now. Stay in it long enough and it ends up defining you, ends up owning you. I've seen it. Always knowing where to be and what do and having all these people around you all thinking and doing things the same way. Watching your back. It's a very easy way to live in many respects. – Pause – Sometimes I can't imagine the type of person I will be when all this is over. What I will do, what I will feel. I know that's a funny thing to say. So it's exciting. But it's scary too.

It sounds very much like you're leaving at the right time, Khalid said. It's always best to leave while you still love a place. You would be surprised at how quickly your passion for a job or a place or a woman or a way of life can turn to bitterness and disillusionment. You have come a long way. You were really only a boy when I first met you.

I was what, twenty-four?

You were still a boy.

Yeah. Maybe.

You put your drink to one side and studied the patterns of the panelling on the ceiling as you spoke. The dice and muffled whump of the ceiling fan unspooling long languorous peels of tobacco smoke.

You know, back then I used to think that there was this *me* before all this; before the soldiering, before the war; and this, this *me* afterwards. That there was some kind of sheer and absolute break separating my life into these two distinct segments that could never touch or meet. The before and after. That the break would always be there, like a scar. Like how the lettering runs all the way through a stick of rock. Cut me open and there'd be this single tree ring right at the centre. – Shrugging your shoulders – I was young. It was a nice illusion to have. It helped make sense of things. Helped give a kind of meaning to everything that happened back then. But the way I see it now…I don't know. The further away from it all I get the more it seems like the war was really just another small part of things, important and unimportant like all the rest. I don't believe in that definite break any more: that's one thing I can say with any certainty. And in a way that makes all this change a lot easier to take. I feel ready for it. But I don't understand things clearly like I used to.

Khalid put two streams of smoke through his nostrils. You sank back onto your elbows.

You are very changed. I can see it. – Nodding to himself several times, tapping the end of his cigarette into an icelime marble ashtray – In my experience the road to maturity is simply the road from the absolute to the unknown. As a child you know nothing. As an adolescent you know everything. And the rest of your life is that slow, difficult process of unlearning all those things you once thought you knew. Maturity is nothing more than the dissolution of belief.

You thought about this. Smiled.

You've got some sort of paradox thing going there, Khale.

Hmm. So I have. I blame the wine. A little on the strong side, isn't it? Makes it rather hard to formulate an incisive line of thought. Or perhaps it's the wine's fault I'm babbling philosophy and aphorisms in the first place, eh? He grunted.

And what about you? Where will you raise the child? Where will you go?

Ha. Now *there* is a question. – Listing the base of the glass between his thumb and forefinger so the ruby sediment caught the light – You know for yourself how troubled the city is. Like it is poised over some terrible precipice, eyes screwed shut against the void. Always reeling between this bright, prosperous future that has been promised us, and a sad spineless slump back into the dark old ways. Have you noticed it? I see it all the time. In the way they still horde their food and supplies like they did when the city was under siege. I see it in the way the women still smuggle make-up to the counter under groceries and papers, how they run their animal eyes in distrust. In the politicians with their cowardly appeasements to sharia for some future elect to ratify and tender them pardon for having ever served under Karzai's blasphemous regime. I see it in the crowds queuing at a checkpoint, talking and laughing and making plans, and not ten feet from them the open casket of an old suicide blast hole. All timeworn and run smooth and dusted at the edges. Just there, just a part of things. You must wonder about the damage that has been done to the collective psyche of a city that has faced everything we have faced. Generational mental scarring. The iniquity of the father visited on the son. Tsk. Who knows. This is not the place for a child, I accept that. But I am nearly an old man and I have a lived here a long time. I was here during the time of the Shah; I was here when they strung up Najibullah's castrated corpse from the traffic signals at Ariana Square after the Russians had abandoned the city; I was here when they murdered Massoud and I remember how that was like the end of hope; and I lived as an exile while they tore my country apart.

Pause.

Where would we go? This is my home. It is too late for me to leave now. I had hoped things would be different, that all the sacrifice and death might have counted for something. But there is only uncertainty ahead.

Pause.

It is a difficult place to raise a child, yes. But I have been a father once already. I let you go to your war after all, didn't I?

He raised his eyes to you under the knotted shelf of his brow and you looked at each other over the table where the emptied glasses were gathered and stained red at the rims and the ashtray smoked and there was only the distant, wiry sound of the sitar.

But enough of all this. – One dismissive flick of his fingers across his face, the brushing away of things that had gathered as he spoke – Tonight we have had good food and good company and ghastly, ghastly wine. We are lucky men to have lived this day.

Yes we are.

Pause.

So tell me. What are your plans before you leave tomorrow?

I have one or two meetings in the morning. Very little to pack.

Have you visited the British cemetery yet? The old Sherpur Cantonment?

No. I meant to when I was last here but I never had the chance.

Tsk. You should go. It is a special place. It understands the city very well.

You nodded.

The old man Rahimullah lives there. He has been there thirty, maybe forty years now. He came to tend the grass with his little flock of sheep decades ago and simply stayed there. He is like the face and conscience of Kabul.

He poured the last of the wine until the grain and silt pooled in the bottle neck.

There is a wonderful story, apocryphal no doubt, that he was once visited by Mullah Omar after the fall of the city, and Omar asked Rahimullah why he dared tend the graves of foreigners and infidel. And Rahimullah replied that at his advanced age he would have less chance of finding a new job than a blind man, apparently forgetting that the eye-patched Omar was, of course, half-blind. And so the cemetery remains.

He drank once. Belched.

While the Taliban were busy tearing down those glorious statues at Bamiyam, busy committing themselves to gutting our history from the very face of the land, this modest little shrine to the outside world somehow went by untouched. Isn't that marvellous?

Pause.

There are many stories buried there. It is a good place to see before you leave. It is a good place to remember. And forget.

You nodded.

It was late. Outside the night was calm and untroubled.

215

A denial of the weight of the past and an indifference to the things yet to come.

You had been against the initial deployment to Kabul from the outset, making your feelings known to the CO in a letter that began Dear Sir, I respectfully request, and had finished with something comically dramatic about you threatening to go AWOL in Vegas, earning you a reply, franked and delivered through official channels despite working in adjoining offices, that began and ended with a brusque Not A Fucking Chance, Yours Aye… But speaking with Khalid that evening you knew the city had captured a part of you and that it held you still though the novelty of your surroundings had long since dimmed. You did not have words sufficient for it, but in some way it comprised great brutality and gentleness existing in unconscious parallel; in poverty that peeled open raw, seemingly boundless yields of resilience and faith and other rare qualities of the human heart that blossomed fiercely from the rubbled country of their brokeness; of age-old mysticism and rumours of dark magic, and of a glorious tapestry of tribal histories snared in an all-too modern war prosecuted by smart missiles and roadside bombs and men in vending-machined air-conditioned offices in distant lands; in the adventure and the stories that seemed to you to lie waiting to be discovered in the simple and the mundane. Finally then, you realised it had captured that part of you because it had shown you beauty again in the most simple of things.

When it was time to leave you stood at the open gates of the compound. There was everything and nothing to be said. And so it went.

Goodbye, old friend.

Goodbye, you said.

You did not turn to meet Khalid's solitary, final wave when you reached the end of the road.

III

You had sat out in a beer garden with Jake late that summer. You had talked about work and then about friends and then about women. The heat from the afternoon carried the kitchen smells out over the patio and beneath them the steady one-note of kerbside exhaust turning itself over in that summer stillness. A spider of sunlight swimming in the shadowed bowl of a wine glass, the light playing off the benchwork making the fibres in the wood stand out in threaded intricacy. And the way the afternoon light seemed to turn the familiar things of the courtyard somehow extraordinary and essential was like an unexpected bloom of hope.

You were quickly at ease with each other. Military jargon and cussing. The cultivated disdain of the soldier towards the rest of the world. There were long pauses in the conversation that did not need to be filled and you looked up at each other in awkward and grateful glances. You had a thirst for the beer. You drank quickly, matching each other, the conversation working in natural turns through pleasantries to complaining to reminiscing, and by only the fourth beer you were honest with each other in the way that drink also makes you honest about the things you have yet to even admit to yourself.

You watched the evening shadows swinging out over the garden and the sun knife-edging the townhouses and then vanishing and the sudden clarity of twilight over the city blowing clean the weight and deadness of the day. Concrete tiles cooling in the breeze. Jake swilled his drink and watched his glass and when you asked him how he was settling back in he had told you shit, I've had more women and food and drink and sleep in the last three months than I ever earned for my troubles out there, and you had both laughed. And he said, don't seem to matter how much I deprive myself of all the good things, I've not yet exhausted my – pause, dramatic emphasis – *monumental* capacity to get it all back in double afterwards and gorge on it until I'm plain sick and desperate to get back out there and starve myself fucking ragged again. You thought it through and you told him that sounded pretty normal. Abstention and indulgence. The same things at play to make a holy man hack chunks out of his spine in contrition or some fat chick sweating and bitching and boasting on day one of her fiftieth diet. Just doled out in different quantities. Guess we're all working for our salvation, right? you had said and Jake had laughed and said, I – pause – *sincerely* hope you're not comparing me to a fat chick, and he had laughed again and then he had gone quiet and he had looked out over your shoulder and for a short while it had been like all those times before when there was nothing that needed to be said and it was enough just to be there.

Then he had told you how he felt like a fraud, coming home a war hero to people who asked him how many men he had killed and who looked at him with new eyes. He told you that he wanted to go back. That it wasn't enough to have been there if you hadn't known combat (not properly, not like you, he added, and you had also somehow felt like a fraud) and that men who had truly known violence were also men who truly knew themselves and that they were men apart, no longer subject to any law or entreaty or moral obligation outside of themselves and that which they had known truly. He told you he felt alone and troubled and homesick for the desert, and then he was quiet and he watched the last of the beer rolling amber and dilute in the bottom of his glass, suddenly conscious of having spoken too easily. It was the first time you had been angry with him for as long as you could remember. Don't go looking for the big pay-off, you had said. It just leaves you cold and empty afterwards. Then you had told him it was distasteful to talk about that stuff and you had half-turned to light a cigarette without turning back.

And you hated yourself for saying all that because you remembered how you too had once hungered for the war. And the real reason you had spoken that way, a reason that would take you many years yet to understand, was because you couldn't bear for someone else to have that which was priceless and sacred to you. How could you have known then that you would give it all up anyway? It was the way of things. You had learned that. You could close your heart up so that it all died out with the memories or you could parcel it out in cheap retellings until there was nothing left. Either way, you lost it all in the end. That struck you cold when you first understood it. But afterwards you wondered how it could be any other way.

The time you had been out by the harbour when the boat backfired. The way everything remained as it was around you and how at the same time it seemed like a loop of film come unscrambled from some cold shadowy part playing out over the surface in confluence: the scene in front of you placid and calm and conditioned with dread like the moments you had known in the worst of battle: each second heightened and strained into superhuman feats of sensitivity, the smallest of movements and sounds processed into a thousand hairtrigger survival strategies. The sun flash on a window like a riflesight glinting off-picture. The leet spilling out to the waterfront or the neat-stacked greenstone harbour walling or the trailers parked up by the mooring stools offering themselves up to you as opportune cover from fire. Diesel fumes that were like your gun sweating out. Feeling yourself bellied-out in indecision by the twin sensations of safety and fear firing away against each other in the most primal and remote places of your brain.

And how afterwards, when the war had already come to seem like something no longer yours, you had thought back to that moment along the harbour, rolling it on your tongue to savour the colours and the smells and the fear. Knowing that in doing so you were also acknowledging that it no longer had dominion over you; and that in this you were also disowning those cool headed and sacred things you had done when they had been necessary. That by honouring the memory you were also laying those things to rest. You had come to learn that our memories and our actions are joined by a fine, pernicious thread and once we have severed the ability of the things we remember to impinge upon our present, we have also severed our joins to the shadows of the person we once were and we have made strange the landscape of our past. It is why we treasure nostalgia even though we know it to be a lie. You had learned that exile from your past is cruel and liberating and inevitable and now, here, standing amongst the gravestones in the quiet of the cemetery garden, looking down at the woodenframed photograph with Bonzo and Woody and Tait and Jonas and Jacko and all the others giving up these big trusting unthinking smiles to a lens that would refute, in long dispassionate years, what had been true in a moment only, you saw that you had returned almost full sweep to that place where you had first began all those years before: an observer, an outsider: no longer an actor in communion with that time and place through the things you had done, but a wanderer in a strange land where there were whispers and reflections and many things hidden from sight. There was a sense of loss that was like old friends taking leave of each other, and it was as much *for* the war as because of it. You had many questions and a lingering sadness and there was very much that you did not understand. You did not understand the war. Its cruelty or its beauty. You did not understand why men have to die.

Looking out over the stones you watched the shadows lean and stretch and turn the thin-cropped grass evening blue, and you watched the wind blowing the tops of the trees so the leaves turned their undersides to you bright and silent and swung away again in ruffled alternate, twin swallows pirouetting in a steep parabola beneath the overhang of the boughs and back up into the curtain of deep, inky starless sky that was just blotting up over the eastern precipice, the last plaintive notes of the call to prayer shivering away in the quiet like a question unanswered, and you watched the old man Rahimullah easing towards the shed hunched double over his cane, nodding to himself with the cane flicking pick-pock-pick-pock over the cobbles and the place in the far wall he passed where there was the mounted plaque saying *we will remember them* with the copperblue tear tracks poured into the wall beneath, and in the cool of the evening you thought about the old man, and about Khalid, and about the city, and about the friends you had known, and about the dead and the living, and you realised the war had only taught you only one thing truly: how wonderful it is to be young, and what a weight of privilege on us left to grow old. And in some small way that made up for the things it had taken from you.

16557900R00136

Printed in Great Britain
by Amazon